The Living Stone

Katie LeMay

ISBN:0995786305
ISBN-13:978-0-9957863-0-1

DEDICATION

To my Mum and Dad.

ACKNOWLEDGMENTS

Thank you to Sara May, who helped edit my book and gave me support to go on with it. As ridiculous as it may sound I found it very difficult to allow anyone to read it in the early days so I thank her for her gentle but honest feedback. I also thank Jenny Lynch whose guidance, and support was invaluable. I thank Lilley Roberts who was kind enough to model as my Inna for my book cover. And last but not least I give thanks to Peter my husband for his patience and support.

CHAPTER ONE

Death is a private affair even for a Queen. Alannis had been thankful for the opportunity to say her last goodbyes to all those people she had wished to speak to in private but there was still one more to come and the time was getting late. Alannis knew there were no more days left and the hours were fast slipping away.

As a Queen she had learnt to be fearless a long time ago but there was one worry weighing heavy on her heart and that was the thought of leaving her beloved granddaughter, she was acutely aware of the enormous responsibilities that would lie ahead of her. If only her daughter were still alive, it would be so different now but if only never solved anything, she scolded herself. This was the way it was. Lithmore was about to have its youngest Queen and the Living Stone would have its youngest Keeper.

She lay in the silence of her room, resting her head upon her pillow seemingly alone, concentrating on the sounds hoping to hear footsteps but everywhere seemed eerily quiet not even the sound of a creaking door or the whistle of the wind could be heard, nothing. Then all of a sudden she heard the rushing sound of movement approaching. The doors to her chamber burst open and a young woman appeared with tears streaming down her face and although regally dressed wearing a beautiful emerald green dress she looked completely dishevelled as the peacock feather headdress she was wearing had fallen lopsided onto the side of her head. The young woman plopped herself into a chair beside Alannis who had managed to raise herself up in her bed and was now looking intently at the sorrowful sight before her, whose tear stained face and her long wavy auburn hair sticking to the side of her cheek, looked such a mess, It was hard to imagine at this moment that this young woman was one of the most beautiful creatures she or anybody else could ever wish to gaze upon..

‘Zelda, dear sweet Zelda, you came.’

‘Oh course I came.’ she sniffed.

She looks so sad thought Alannis, not her usual vivacious, flamboyant self. There had only been one other occasion she had seen Zelda so upset, they had both cried that day when the news had arrived that her only child had been killed. The pain of that memory remained fresh in her mind. She had lost a daughter and Zelda a best friend. Strange bonds come out of grief and through the years that followed Zelda had made the pain of losing Xania more bearable for Alannis.

‘I can't believe you are leaving us.’ Zelda protested.

‘It is time my dear, my body is spent. I can hear my ancestors calling me.’

‘Tell them they will have to wait. We need you here with us.’

Alannis chuckled, there was something very endearing and innocent about Zelda. She was the perfect choice for the job.

‘I can't bear to lose you. I just can't bear it.’ Once again the tears began to fall.

Alannis patted Zelda's hand comforting her and couldn't resist smiling to herself at the irony of the situation.

‘I need you to listen to me. I need your help. I am concerned for my beloved Inna.'

Zelda stopped crying and looked towards Alannis attentively. Inna being Xania's daughter already held a special place in Zelda's heart and there was nothing that she would not do for her.

'It is a daunting enough task to become Queen but for Inna she is also going to be the new Keeper of the Living Stone.' Alannis sighed, concern appearing on her face.

'She is so young.' Zelda cupped Alannis hand and gave it a gentle squeeze.

'How can I help?'

Finally, thought Alannis, she is listening to me. Bless her.

'Inna has been well trained in her duties but she will need guidance in becoming a woman and that dear heart is where you come in. I need you to be her mother, sister, teacher, and friend. She already loves and adores you. Will you be willing to take the role of Inna's guardian?

'I can do that,' Zelda answered brightly.

'It will mean leaving your precious Newel, you will have to live here for the most part. Are you willing to do that?'

'For you I can do anything and for the memory of Xania I will do it for her also.'

Alannis knew there was no one better to entrust Inna to, she felt confident that Zelda would give her the love and support she would need in the future. For one so young her new roles required wisdom beyond her years, a quick discerning mind, the ability to judge the hearts of men and at all times she would need to contain a great deal of love and compassion for the people she served. Yes, thought Alannis she was going to need Zelda's strength and her zany sense of humor to help her through.

It had been difficult seeing Zelda for the last time, goodbyes were never easy, now dawn was beginning to awaken the world. Alannis's small failing figure lay upon her white circular bed, she could feel the time getting closer, death was calling her but she did not feel any fear. There was only one other person there in the chamber with her and he had been there all night sitting quietly as he was now, looking out through the open doors onto the balcony, with its view that reached out across the sea and as he breathed in he could smell the salt air. Now he gazed around the room he could not help but contemplate that Alannis had chosen a perfect place to end her life; her bed lay over a large hexagram made of Malachite, the colour of emerald green, White shiny marble covered the remainder of the floor. A large fireplace dominated the room, although seldom used; it had been lit today as Alannis was feeling the cold. Hiliron, for that was his name, continued to behold the view beyond the balcony. He stood with his shoulders slightly slumped watching the fishermen returning home after their nights fishing, lines of worry more apparent upon his ageing face, the normal twinkle in his eye replaced by a sadness and a knowing of what was to come and inside he felt angry. The seagulls gathered around the little boats, screeching loudly calling out to others to join them in their feast. Rotten little scavengers, thought Hiliron, he was not very fond of seagulls, they made far too much noise for his liking and he felt the smaller birds never stood a chance at the tit bits.

The sound of Alannis's breathing deep and laboured, begins to fill the room.

'Hiliron.' she calls out, her voice weak and rasping.

His thoughts interrupted, Hiliron turns towards the frail old women.

'I am so cold.' Her voice is almost a whisper.

He tenderly pulls the sheep skin cover up over her, as he does so he gazes into her face. A flash of their youth springs into his memory and he feels his heart begin to race a little faster and he aches for the times he can never have again. Releasing a sigh, knowing time is running out. He begins to prepare the room. First he lights the torches that hang on the walls around the room, then he closes the shutters to prevent the light from the outside world from creeping in. Lastly he makes his way over to the hearth and begins piling more wood onto the fire. When all is done he sweeps a keen eye over his work and satisfied all is as it should be, he turns towards Alannis and unashamedly climbs his tall aged frame upon the bed to lie beside her. For now, just in this instance, Alannis was not only his Queen but also his beloved companion. The thought of her leaving him leaves a cold emptiness deep inside him that he feels will never be warmed again. In this moment she is just his Alannis, he gently wraps his arms around her pulling her closer to him, as he softly kissers her cheek. No words are spoken; all that had to be said had long been said. This was a time for holding and embracing, for remembering, for just one last time together. Alannis released a gentle sigh. She too was appreciating the moment. Her breathing appeared less laboured and peaceful. The room now seemed very still and almost dark with the exception of the fire and the few torches Hiliron had lit, the small flames dancing, creating shadows on the wall. Only the crackling sounds from the fire and Alannis's steady breathing could be heard.

The two lay cradled together blissfully for some time until Alannis began to stir, squeezing Hiliron's arm with her frail bony hand. She whispered.

'It's time. Is everything prepared?'

'Yes my love. Everything is ready.'

Hiliron gave a slight cough as to clear his throat. Suddenly he felt very tense. His neck tightened and felt restricted. His heart sank, yet he managed to force a smile when Alannis spoke.

'Then it is time to bring her to me.'

Hiliron kissed her once more and gathered himself off the bed. Slowly he collected his silver staff that had lain by the chair. His once handsome face now old and creased by the lines of time, looked strained, his deep set brown eyes that always appeared to hold the wisdom of the world now flickered lost and unsure. For a moment there was silence as Hiliron stood by the door looking back at the only women he had ever loved.

'Hiliron,' Alannis called to him, her voice weak.
'You know, I shall always be there, - waiting until you come.'

'I know,' he said fighting back the tears and with a heavy sigh he opened the chamber door and pounded his staff onto the floor sending a resounding echo throughout the room. Seconds later a tall youth appeared at the door looking about seventeen years of age with wild black uncontrollable hair, wearing bright red linen trousers, his chest bare revealing his bronzed skin. His eyes, the colour of midnight widened as he entered the room.

'Teka my boy. We need you to fetch Inna to us.'

Hiliron spoke softly but with authority. Teka quickly glanced over to the frail woman lying on the bed and for a moment he felt overwhelming sadness, for he liked the old woman, oh he loved her as his Queen, but he liked her, she had been a great listener and story teller to him as he was growing up. She had always been so full of life and young looking, that was the reward of being the Keeper of the Stone it kept you looking young, but the decaying old woman that Teka saw before him was not the same woman he had seen a few days before.

'You must not waste time bringing her to us, the time is now. Do you understand?'

'Yes, yes,' Teka stammered nervously.

'I will go right away.' Teka turned to leave when he heard the old woman call out to him.

'Teka,...Teka my boy, come here, come closer. I have something to say to you.'

Apprehensively, Teka crossed the room to be close to Alannis. He knelt down beside her.

'Don't look so grieved boy, my body has given up not my soul, I am just going on a new journey that is all. It is the goodbyes' that are painful and that is why I need your help. Inna will need your love and support. You are her best friend, and she will need you close in the days to come. Say you will be there for her Teka.'
The old woman grabbed Teka's hand.

The fear that had struck Teka when he first arrived into the room disappeared and a gentle smile grew on his face as he dared to cover his Queens hand with his,

'Beloved Alannis.,' he said, sounding much older than is age.

'Don't you know? My soul's purpose is to always be by Inna's side. I would give my life for her.'

Alannis smiled and gently patted the side of Teka's face.

'Bless you my son. Go now and bring her to me.'

*****

Teka found Inna in the Temple gardens and for a moment he stood silently in the shade of one of the willow trees just watching undetected. How he loved her. He could hear her talking.

'My lovelies would you like some water this fine bright day, or are you content as you are?'

She was directing her question to the flowers in the garden; in her hand she held a vessel with a spout. With some of the flowers she bent down and poured water onto them and others she passed them by as if having asked the question they had answered and replied no to her.

Teka watched while she stretched her growing body. She was already a beauty with her hair as black as night, her olive skin glistened in the sunlight from under the white thin cotton dress that she wore. Her long athletic legs were visible. On her feet she wore simple leather sandals. It was not her cherry bud lips or her tiny turned up nose that Teka loved the most but her eyes, they were as blue as the sea and when she looked at you, it was as if she could see into your soul. Absolutely captivating, thought Teka, no wonder everyone loves her, she will make a good Keeper of the Living Stone and be a much loved Queen.

As if someone nudged his thoughts he realized it was time to take her away from this special place known as the temple garden, where everything flourished even under the hot sun. Flowers bloomed all year round creating a mass of colour upon the ground. Pools of water, deep enough to swim in, were so clear you could see the sand at the bottom. Trees swayed gently in the breeze creating umbrellas of shade to lie under. It was truly a magical place where priests and priestesses, healers and tellers, poets and artists could come and be inspired, rejuvenated, or to simply contemplate; whatever their needs, the garden seemed to fulfil.

'Inna,' Teka spoke softly. Inna turned towards the voice and saw Teka standing near the willow tree.

'Go away Teka,' Inna's face looked sullen; she continued to water the flowers.

'Inna, I have been sent to fetch you.' Teka continued.

'I don't care, go away.' Inna's mouth fixed in a pout and she continued to ignore him.

'Hiliron has sent me, it's time. Your Grandmother needs you.'

Inna placed the vessel onto the ground and sighed heavily.

‘I know, I just don't want it to be,’ she said, finally acknowledging Teka.

‘I can't bear the thought of losing her, let alone know how I shall cope without her. The task before me seems so big to bear.’

Teka could see the liquid increase in her eyes and watched helplessly as a tear fell unguardedly down her face. He pulled her to him and held her for a moment.

‘I am afraid, Teka.’

‘I know, but you can do this, you must,’ he squeezed her tightly then gently pushing her away from him he swept her long black hair behind her small petite ears and gently wiped the tears from her face. Inna inhaled deeply.

‘Ok, I am ready.’

Lifting Inna's hand slowly to his mouth, Teka gently caressed his lips onto the back of her hand with a gentle kiss as though an agreement had just been made.

‘Come on, brave girl, you can do this.’

Silently they walked hand in hand through the gardens, back into the palace hurriedly making their way along the corridors towards Alannis's chamber. People stopped when they spotted the two of them and bowed their heads in respect. Everyone was aware their Queen was dying and seeing Inna and Teka walking in such a rushed manner could only mean one thing that the time was near.

Arriving outside the chamber Inna pauses briefly, her eyes eagerly searching Teka's for guidance but he only kisses her cheek and pushes her towards the door.

Inside the room Hiliron is holding the failing Alannis in his arms; he gently carries her over to in front of the hearth then lovingly puts her down in front of the blazing fire, and places pillows behind her back to allow her to sit comfortably. Suddenly the door burst open and Inna rushes into the room.

'Oh Grandmother,' she cries, and runs towards the tiny figure collapsing to her knees on the floor beside her.

Alannis gently begins to stroke Inna's head.

'The time is now child; I only have a few more breaths in me'

Inna gazes into her Grandmother's eyes, terrified at the thought of losing her, frightened of the responsibilities that lay ahead. This is it, she thought. I can't stop what is about to happen. Sitting up she crosses her legs to face her Grandmother, her heart now thumping madly inside her chest as she tries to force a smile to indicate that she is ready for the initiation to begin, but for a moment Alannis turns her attention away from Inna and says.

'Hiliron, before you go, please pass me the tools for the initiation.' Surprisingly her voice sounds stronger.

Hiliron crosses the room and opens a chest that is tucked in the corner, opening it; he pulls out a box wrapped in a purple velvet cloth. He returns to Alannis and places it into her lap. Grabbing his hand she speaks to him for the last time.

'Thank you Hiliron. That is all. You may take your leave now.'

Their eyes lock momentarily; Hiliron gently takes the old woman's hand and kisses it then turns towards Inna and kisses the top of her forehead. Looking at them both he says,

'May peace and joy be with you through your transitions,' and without another word he slowly makes his way to the door. Neither one could feel his heartbreak or see his tears uncontrollably fall upon his face as he left the dim lit chamber.

CHAPTER TWO

As the fire crackled the room felt warm and cosy. Inna always felt safe whenever she was with her beloved Grandmother and this time was no different although today was no ordinary day and for the first time she felt a little apprehensive in her presence.

'Inna,' the old women whispered.

'You know the time is now. We must proceed with the initiation.'

Inna nodded her head, her eyes as big as saucers. She reached out and covered her hand over her beloved Grandmother's.

'I love you my Grandmother.' Tears began to fall down her face as she tried to speak.

'Don't be frightened dear child; it is only my body that will leave you. My spirit will remain with you always.'

Alannis smiled reassuringly as she looked into the anxious face of Inna.

'This is a celebration as well as an initiation. Let us take some deep calming breaths.'

Slowly and gently the two females began to inhale deeply, exhaling through their mouths. At first Inna fidgeted and kept scooping her hair behind her ears, a habit she had whenever she felt overwhelmed. I must concentrate; she chastised herself, and then decided to close her eyes. Within a few minutes she could feel a stillness begin to descend into the room, everything seemed to suddenly feel very calm and peaceful, even the fire burned quietly, she could hear no other external noises, just the in and out of their breathing.

After a while Alannis touched Inna's knee to get her attention then placed the contents Hiliron had given her between herself and Inna and began unraveling the purple cloth revealing a wooden box. Reaching inside, she pulled out a small round tin bowl and placed it between them.

'Pass me the sage Inna. We will burn it in the bowl. This will allow us to call upon our ancestors for they have to be present at this ceremony, it will also purify the room.'

Inna quickly handed the sage to her Grandmother's outstretched hand who placed it into a bowl and lit the leaves with a flame then she began to exhale her breath slowly and deliberately, blowing the smoke from the sage out into the room.

'Now you take the bowl Inna and go around the room and do exactly as I have just done but make sure you blow the sage into the corners, it will get rid of any negative energy.'

Inna took the bowl and did as her Grandmother asked then returned to face her once again, meanwhile her Grandmother had began to chant a tune, her voice suddenly stronger and as beautiful as it ever was. Inna began to feel a little dazed as though she was falling into a trance. For a moment she closed her eyes, savouring the sound of her voice, when she opened them again a group of women surrounded her, some looked remarkably like herself others looked much older. The older women had exquisite white hair and wore lilac silk robes; the young ones all had long black hair and wore white robes. They were all smiling at Inna greeting her but not saying a word, yet Inna understood what they were saying, no words were necessary.

'As you can see my dear child, our ancestors have come to join us on this most important occasion. Soon I will be with them. As you see them now, so will you see me. Do you understand now, that I will always be with you?'

'Yes, I think I do,' Inna stumbled over her words.

Alannis reached into the box again and this time pulled out a necklace made of clear quartz in the shape of a star, its points were rounded and delicate making it a beautiful piece, Alannis handed the necklace to Inna and said,

'This crystal must be worn by you at all times, when there is nowhere to turn and your need is great you may hold this quartz up to the light of the sun or of a flame and I shall come to you. Also this crystal can talk to you. Ask it questions and be silent, your answers may come in a dream or a vision but they will come, trust and believe and the crystal will be a great friend to you.'

Inna took the necklace.

'Thank you Grandmother,'

she placed the necklace around her neck. All the ancestors in the room smiled their approval.

One of the older women steps forward and bending down she passes a small vile to Alannis who thanks her.

'This is my mother Inna. She has given me the special magical powder that only Keepers of the Stone may take. Open your mouth child.'

Inna did as she was asked and opened her mouth. Her Grandmother poured the powder under her tongue.

'This will help you to see into men's hearts, to know the truth, and it will allow you to read men's minds, this gift must not be abused and you must decide wisely when to use it . Now to your voice, as you know each day you must sing to the Living Stone for this is its food. It is the sound from your voice that will help to resonate the healing energies within the heart of the stone. It is what keeps the stone alive. Through the years you have had much training to prepare you for this day. Taking the powder will activate your voice to the correct frequency that is needed for the survival of the stone.'

Inna felt an instant tingling in the back of her throat, it wasn't unpleasant but she found herself swallowing several times to try and clear the sensation.

Alannis leant forward once more and reached into the box and pulled out a small golden sphere, for a moment she paused and glanced around the room, as if taking one last look, then rested her smiling eyes upon Inna. She began to utter words that Inna could not understand, the other women joined in, their voices getting louder and louder until finally Alannis drew the sphere to her third eye, her breathing laboured, her body began to convulse. Inna was filled with terror, as she watched helplessly, she could see a swirling haze like a vortex covering her Grandmother's forehead and within this vortex, Inna could see images of so many things moving so fast, pictures of events that she remembered with her Grandmother and of things she knew nothing about, unsure what was happening for a moment, then panicking as she realized her beloved Grandmother was sucking her own life force from her body.

'No, No,' she could hear her voice cry,

but there was no time to think, no time to feel, as Alannis quickly passed Inna the golden sphere, instinctively she placed it onto her third eye. Overwhelming feelings of love and compassion flooded her whole being; all fear swept away, she felt and was in a state of ecstasy. A golden mist rotated around her transforming into all the colours of the rainbow. Inna wanted the feeling to last forever; she gazed at her Grandmother who was now slumped over, lifeless. Inna looked up to her ancestors and there she was standing amongst them, smiling down at her.

The initiation was complete. Strangely at that moment she feels no grief but a total feeling of peace, and overwhelmingly tired. She lays down on the carpet, her eyelids heavy she forcers herself to glance up towards her Grandmother, wanting to see her face one last time but she is too late the chamber is now completely empty. She surrenders to the desire to close her eyes and within moments quickly drifts off into a deep and peaceful sleep.

The following morning all is quiet in the palace. Hiliron enters the chamber to find Alannis's dead body where he had left her, still in a sitting position, beside her; Inna lays stretched out upon the rug sleeping. Hiliron is full of love for both of them. A sharp pain hits his chest as the realization sinks in that his precious Alannis is no more, and he wonders how he will cope without having her close to him, how lonely will his days be.

Shaking his head, so many loved ones no longer here, he was getting old, too old he thought, when would it be his time to go? He took a swift intake of breath as though chastising himself for his self-pitying. Young Inna was going to need him in the coming days as she adjusts to her new role. He brushed a tear from his eyes and gently bent to touch Inna's arm.

‘Inna,’ he whispered.

‘Inna, it is time to wake up. There is much work to be done.’

Inna opened her eyes, she felt wonderful after her deep sleep, she smiled up at Hiliron who noticed her peaceful face change to sadness as the reality dawned on her that her Grandmother was no longer with them. Her mind confused, she turned to Hiliron.

‘What must I do, Hiliron?’

‘We must prepare for the funeral it will be a grand occasion with many emissaries coming from all over the world to say their goodbyes, but first you must attend to the Living Stone.’

‘But I am not sure I am ready.’

Suddenly she was consumed with panic. Hiliron could see in her eyes that she was frightened. He reached down and pulled Inna to her feet and hugged her to him.

'You are ready my child, all will be well, remember your breathing it will calm you. Now go.' He gently led her to the door.

As she was leaving she turned once more toward Hiliron but he said nothing, he just gently nodded his head in assurance.

CHAPTER THREE

Inna felt numb as she walked along the corridors with their vast columns painted elaborately with hieroglyphics, the bright colours normally uplifted her mood but not today she was finding it hard to imagine how life was going to be without her Grandmother. The sensation of being alone was new to her and it was frightening.

Where is everybody, she thought irritably, normally at this time she would have passed dozens of people by now, then she realized the citizens of Lithmore would not leave their homes today, the whole city would be in mourning, their day would be spent praying for their old Queen to have a safe and easy entrance to the next life, this was the custom of her people. Each household will place a lantern outside their door a sign that a death had occurred in their family, in this case everyone's family as it is their Queen who is dead.

At the entrance of the great hall Inna could see a lone figure and recognised him as old Nao, one of the temple artists. At first he does not hear Inna approach; pausing beside him for a moment she calls,

'Good day.'

The old man looks up and gives a quick nod of his head acknowledging her presence then continues with his painting. Inna was in awe of the artists that painted the hieroglyphics on the walls and columns and even the extremely tall obelisk that stood at the entrances of Lithmore she had often thought how dangerous it must be for the men who perform these duties, sometimes they needed to work many feet up in the air to reach their work and many of them were not young. Thankfully she had never heard of any of them coming to any harm. Inna's whole life was painted on these walls as was her mother's and Grandmother's before her; in fact the whole of Lithmore's history was illustrated for all to see.

Today old Nao was relaying the passing of her Grandmother, she recognised herself in the picture and Hiliron and when her eyes rested on Hiliron immediately her thoughts were brought back to the present and to her duties, she entered the mystical garden quickening her pace as she went. In the distance she could see the entrance to the Living Stone and once again she could feel her hands getting sweaty and her heart begin to race. I am only fifteen, for goodness sake; this should not be happening to me, I'm too young for such a huge responsibility. Inna stopped walking to try and calm herself; she was standing beside the statue of the first Keeper of the Stone. Without realizing it Inna spoke out loud to the marbled girl.

‘Help me, please give me courage.’

The first keeper of the stone had been not much older than herself, in her hand she held a copy of the sceptre her Grandmother had used during the initiation and she was pointing it. Inna stared at her and realized she was pointing it directly at the building that housed the Living Stone.

‘Thanks, you're a lot of help.’

Inhaling a deep breath and forcefully blowing it out, she slowly places one foot in front of the other towards the chamber door.

Immediately Inna feels chilled as she enters the building, she no longer has the warm protection of the sun to comfort her. The walls are made of thick stone, no fires burn in these corridors.

She quickens her pace to prevent herself from shivering. At the entrance of the chamber, she is greeted by two guards, one standing each side of the doorway, young strong men dressed in white linen tunics exposing half of their upper bodies revealing their youthful muscles. Inna recognises them both right away; they are Niko and Milo, two young guards she has known all her life. Immediately the two men bow their heads, which makes Inna flush with embarrassment as she has never been bowed to before. That honour was only given to the Queen but now she was Queen she was not so sure she cared for such protocol, however she was pleased to see both of them, somehow she was reassured by their presence. Milo stepped forward to open the door for her. This is it, she thought, there is no going back now. She took a deep breath, the two young men looked at one another, they wanted to tell her they were rooting for her that she was going to be all right but they both knew it was not their place to do so, so instead they both smiled reassuringly which somehow seemed to give Inna the strength she needed.

'I am ready now. You can open the door please.'

The young Queen inhaled a deep breath and entered into the chamber of the Living Stone.

Once inside, she was surprised at the immediate change she felt from stepping inside the room, it felt as if all her anxiety just slipped away and now she was feeling calm and confident, how odd she thought. She could see that the room was lit by several candles and that the room was circular in shape as were many of the rooms in the temple. Her eyes were drawn to the centre of the room to where the Living Stone lay.

'Welcome,' a voice spoke,

Inna looked around the room to see who was there.

'Welcome,' the voice spoke again.

There was no one else here, Inna was sure of it. Where was the voice coming from? The stone began pulsating light into the room.

'Come closer my child.'

Oh my, thought Inna, it is the stone, the stone is speaking to me.

'Come closer, so you can connect to the music.'

Inna had seen the Living Stone many times, but she had never heard it speak, and she had never seen such energy radiating from it before. Intrigued, she stepped forward to be closer to the stone. Very faintly at first she began to hear music, beautiful music, it got louder and louder and as it did so she felt light headed and floaty and before she knew it her feet were no longer touching the ground, she was actually floating in the air, then came this magnificent powerful exquisite sound like an angel singing, to her delight and amazement she realized it was her own voice, she was singing to the stone, she was really singing to the stone. The words had come as her Grandmother promised they would.

'Deno comtu les me om, deno comtu les me om. Far lo mor deno comtu les me om.
Comtu les me on.

Which meant breathe life into me, breathe life into me forever more, breathe life to me.

Glorious colours swirled around the room. Inna felt such euphoria. Why? She thought had she been so afraid to come here, this was such an honour. The music began to fade and slowly Inna descended until her feet touched the ground she found herself embracing the stone, humbled by the experience. The rich voice of the stone spoke once again.

'Thank you Inna. You are destined to be a good Keeper.'

All the anxieties that she had felt before she entered the room had been completely washed away. Now she was sure she would be able to cope with being Queen and Keeper of the Stone, she now knew that the stone would give her strength.

Lithmore was a great city because of the Living Stone. People from faraway lands travelled to receive healing from the stone. Its magical powers were capable of curing the most deadly diseases and people from far and wide knew this so they would travel weeks and months to arrive at Lithmore just for the chance to touch the stone, with them they brought trade and revenue thus making Lithmore a very wealthy city. None of the training Inna's Grandmother had given her had really prepared her for this moment, she had always been tormented by the thought of becoming the new Keeper of the Living Stone and was not too keen on being Queen but now, everything seemed to fit into place, it was as if the stone had given her an inner strength and a confidence she never thought possible. She patted the stone fondly saying,

'Until the next time, thank you.

CHAPTER FOUR

Lithmore was alive with the hustle and bustle of people preparing for the funeral. Strangers and friends alike came flooding through the large city gates in a constant stream. Everyone eager to pay their last respects to their beloved Queen and Keeper of the Stone.

City folk were opening up their homes to offer food and shelter to strangers while hundreds of people walked the streets patiently waiting for sunset. The important dignitaries were provided with rooms within the palace and many of these people were now gathered in the great hall.

Hiliron and Inna spent most of the morning finalising last minute arrangements for the funeral then later joined their guests in the hall but it wasn't long before the noise and chatter of the people assembled there began to overwhelm Inna, eagerly she scanned the room for Teka, desperately needing someone familiar by her side. She still had not had a chance to see or speak to Zelda who was involved in preparing her Grandmother's body for the funeral. Inna's head began to throb and to make matters worse she had been cornered by an elderly couple who were heaping a list of complaints upon her about the inefficiency of their accommodation. All the time Inna felt like screaming, this is a funeral, make do and mend. There is no pleasing some people, she thought. The final straw came when she heard the old man say.

'You really should put more thought into these ceremonies beforehand.'

Really! I have to get out of here, thought Inna, if I don't I am going to scream, so smiling as sweetly as she could muster she made her excuses and disappeared as fast as she could out into the corridor and kept walking until she found herself out onto the streets of Lithmore.

There were just as many people in the city but none of them were demanding her attention nor did they seem to recognise her. She breathed the air in and began to stroll along stopping here and there to watch the festivities because, although this was a funeral day, it was also considered a day of celebration and the streets were full of dancers, magicians and singers. All sorts of entertainments were taking place and, unlike the previous few days, the market stalls were all busy working. At one of the stalls, the old man recognised Inna instantly and offered her a freshly baked piece of buttered bread, she took it gratefully, and the aroma somehow reminded her she had not eaten in a very long time. She thanked him for his kind gift and continued to wander aimlessly around the city until she saw a familiar face running towards her, it was Teka and he did not look very happy. Breathing heavily he stood slightly bent forward trying to regain his breath.

'Inna, where have you been? What do you think you are doing coming out into the street like this?'

Inna, felt slightly perplexed by Teka's harsh tone,

'I just needed to get away for a while.'

'Hiliron wants you. There are many important people waiting to meet you,' and without waiting for a response he grabbed Inna's hand and began to make his way through the crowd with her.

'What's wrong, Teka, why are you being so mean?' Teka stopped abruptly and swung around to face her.

'Don't you know?' Then looking into her puzzled face he could see she did not.

'No you don't do you. Well, my dear, dear Inna. You can no longer be that carefree girl of a few days ago. You are now the Queen of

Lithmore and Keeper of the Living Stone. You are going to be much loved all of your life but my dear heart, there are those few that won't be so keen on you for one reason or another and they may be those scheming to harm you as we speak,' Teka sighed.

'We were worried when we could not find you.'

Inna bit her bottom lip; she had been selfish she had not given it any thought. Her only instinct had been to get away from everyone; she had only wanted a moment to herself.

'I am sorry Teka,- it's just.' Then she threw her arms around his neck and for a moment they embraced.

'Friends again?'

'Friends, now come on we have to get back.'

Many more people had gathered by the time Inna and Teka returned to the great hall. Zelda spotted Inna and immediately floated across the room towards her. Men stepped aside with longing in their eyes and women gave gentle curtseys with envy in their hearts at the breathtaking beauty wafting past them. Zelda, as always, was oblivious that anyone was paying the least bit of attention to her. With arms outstretched and aiming for Inna, she threw her arms around her new ward in a firm embrace.

'My poor sweet girl!' she exclaimed.

'So young, so much responsibility, I tried to warn your Grandmother but she would not listen, she thought she would live forever, silly old goat, now she has gone and died on us, but you're not to worry my darling, I will be here to look after you.'

Inna could hardly breathe, Zelda was squeezing her so tight she thought her bones would break.

'I am so glad you're here,' Inna managed to say.

‘Let me take a good look at you.’ At last, Inna could breathe again.

‘Yes, I think you have grown another inch since I last saw you.

She tilted her head to one side and regarded Inna.

‘You know, you are becoming quite a beauty young lady.’

Inna could not stop the flush of colour rising into her cheeks but she was delighted to finally be with Zelda whom she adored, she was always such fun to be around, her stunning good looks drew the attention of everyone around her who admired her beautiful walnut coloured hair and stunning emerald green eyes, not to mention her zany sense of humor that never failed to cause a smile on Inna's face.

‘Grandmother told me you will be helping Hiliron guide me, won't you miss Newell?’

‘Yes of course I will, but we will visit as much as possible.’

‘I am so sorry you have to leave your home,’

Inna was feeling sad, she hated the thought of ever having to leave Lithmore.

‘Don’t look so tragic it is not as if I am leaving any children behind or a man,’ Zelda threw her head back and laughed.

‘You will be my family from now on, that is what your dear Grandmother wanted for both of us.’

Inna was beginning to see what it was that her Grandmother and Zelda had in common, they were both loving people and, although Zelda could be loud and flamboyant from time to time and was even known to be somewhat of a drama queen, her compassion for others was real. Inna felt a hand on her elbow, it was Teka.

‘Hiliron wishes to speak with you,’ he whispered in her ear.

Inna looked across the hall to where Hiliron sat; he was taking council with a group of men, having got Inna's attention he now waved her over to him.

'We have some important guests from the south land's that would like to meet you.'

Inna by nature was a shy girl and, although she loved people, she was always more comfortable in the company of animals and nature. She was fine and happy with those she knew but it was always difficult for her to meet new people. Now she had been pushed into a role where this would be a common occurrence, a daily event, she would have to get used to small talk which she absolutely hated and learn to chitchat about nothing in particular and learn to listen with a discerning ear. Oh dear, she thought, nothing is ever easy but, to Inna's surprise, as the afternoon went on she found herself slipping into the role very well and it was not nearly the task she thought it was going to be, she found the people interesting and pleasing and very kind to her. Many of them had known her Grandmother well and relayed stories she had never heard before, often making her laugh. They in turn were thrilled to be able to share their memories with her.

As sunset approached people began to prepare for the funeral procession when suddenly, to everyone's surprise, a kerfuffle broke out at the entrance to the great hall, raised murmurs turned quickly into shouting. A deep roaring voice could be heard above all the others. Inna heard her name mentioned. Zelda grabbed Inna's hand and pulled her protectively towards her. Hiliron rose from his chair to face the booming voice, people pulled aside as a tall blond man with an alarming presence stomped across the great hall towards Hiliron. Inna observed his outward appearance; he clearly horrified the surrounding guests. His tatty torn cloths were dirty and he was unshaven, he looked like he had not bathed in some time. A group of guards came bursting in behind the intruder just as the stranger and Hiliron came face to face. Hiliron stood erect staring straight at him, his jaw fixed, he was clearly not pleased to see this interloper.

'Calem the Transporter.' Hiliron bellowed not showing the least bit of fear. Inna was very impressed. Everyone else seemed terrified of the intruder.

'Have you no shame to come here at this hour?' continued Hiliron.

'I want to see the Keeper of the Stone.' The stranger's voice was rough and demanding.

People close by began to cower away, Inna could sense their fear. Who is he? Thought Inna, his eyes so dark and menacing, but there was something about him, something that intrigued her, what was he doing here at this hour?

'Who is he?' whispered Inna.

'Hush little one, I will tell you later,' replied Zelda.

'You have no right to ask for the Keeper of the Stone today. Today she is our Queen, a Queen who is about to bury another Queen, her role as Keeper of the Stone is secondary at this moment in time.'

The stranger ignored Hiliron.

'I repeat,' his voice became louder and more demanding.

'I want to see the Keeper of the Stone and I insist that I see her now.'

Hiliron, generally a very placid man, frowned and gritted his teeth. He felt his fists begin to clinch, not normally a violent man by nature, he suddenly had the urge to swing for this troublesome trespasser. Seeing Hiliron's face and fearing what he might do next Inna stepped forward.

'What do you want of me?' she found herself looking directly into his eyes, surprisingly she felt no fear.

'Have you no respect for the hour. What is so important that you have the bad manners to interrupt our proceedings?'

To everyone's surprise Calem the Transporter looked embarrassed and, for a moment, seemed uncertain of what to say next.

'My people,' he managed to say,

'Many of my people are sick, several are dead already. I know the stone can help them.'

Inna thought for a moment.

'What form does this illness take?'

'See for yourself. '

Calem stepped aside to reveal a young boy about seven years old, he called him to his side, and the little boy limped towards him in obvious pain, his face full of sores. The crowd gasped and retreated as far back as possible.

'It is not catching you morons,' Calem lifted the boy protectively to him.

'Can you be sure this illness can't be spread to others?'

'I am sure. Everyone got sick on the same day and no one else has shown any signs of illness since.'

'I see, it seems as if they have all consumed a poison of some kind.'

Hiliron nodded his head in agreement.

'Yes, I think I must agree with you.'

'Have you brought all your sick to Lithmore?' Continued Inna.

'Yes. We know the stone is our last hope.'

Inna regarded Calem for a moment. This was a good man, a little rough maybe but nevertheless a good man.

'I will help you Calem the Transporter but first we must proceed with the funeral. Do you think you can wait just a little while longer until we have chance to bury my Grandmother?'

Calem nodded his head, relieved; at last, he now felt real hope for his people. Bowing his head to the young girl he turned to Hiliron and gave a short sharp nod. Hiliron softened his jaw after hearing of Calem's plight and inwardly smiled to himself thinking how proud Alannis would have been of Inna, she certainly had her Grandmothers touch with people.

'Until after the funeral then, thank you,' and with that he turned and left with the small boy and the rest of his followers.

As soon as they had gone the great hall erupted to the sound of excited conversation. Inna immediately turned to Zelda.

'Quick Zelda tell me who is that man?'

'That, dear child, is Calem the Transporter and, if the stories are true about him, he is a murderer and a thief.'

'And that is exactly what they are, stories. We don't know for sure if they are true,' corrected Hiliron.

'But what we do know about him is he is a great warrior although somewhat unorthodox in his methods. He was heavily involved in putting an end to the Krugen rising about five years ago but, more importantly, what you might like to know about him is he has the gift of transporting.'

'Wow you mean he can transport himself or anything to any place in the blink of an eye?'

Both Zelda and Hiliron nodded their heads.

'One moment he can be standing in a room with you and the next he can be in another country.'

'Wow, I thought they were only myths, I did not know anyone could actually do that. So where is he from?'

'Oh he is a Drugan, his people live in the far north, hence the blond hair. They all have blond hair from up north.'

How fascinating thought Inna, and in that instance a strange feeling swept over her that this man was going to have some bearing on her life, although she could not think what connection they could possibly have with each other. At that moment her thoughts were interrupted by the loud sound of a gong, it was the announcement that the funeral was about to begin.

Thousands of people lined the pavements for their last farewell to their beloved Queen. Six men carried her body through the streets, towards the temple gates. Inna, Zelda and Hiliron walked behind the small coffin. Inna kept her head bowed with her eyes constantly staring toward the ground. She could hear the crowds, some crying some calling out Alannis's name; others threw flowers onto the street in front of the procession. From time to time Inna forced herself to look up, the people were so close she could see their faces, so many different people, some had blond hair, they must be from up north she thought, their skin so pale in comparison to hers. Another group of people were like giants so tall holding their heads erect, how very proud they looked.

The sun was going down but the heat of the day was still very uncomfortable. Inna found herself fascinated by the different reactions she saw in the people, some were deathly quite as the procession walked past, others cheered as in celebration, yet others wailed and cried. How different we all are she thought. Death causes us all to react in so many different ways, she herself just felt numb. She did not fear death, as she knew it was merely a stepping out of one body to pass into another whether that is physical or a spiritual body it did not matter because she believed the essence of herself continued but in a changed form. She knew this to be true as she had seen for herself, the night of the initiation, when her ancestors had visited her. She had also seen her Grandmother leave her body and join those that had gone before.

The procession came to a halt as they arrived at the foot of the temple steps, the trumpet sounds got louder and a constant beating of drums drowned out the noise of the people. Then everything fell deathly silent. Alannis was within a short journey to her final resting place. The six men began to climb the steps, struggling to make the journey as smooth as possible, each one determined not to let the other down, fearing humiliation and disgrace if they should allow the beautifully hand woven seagrass gasket to fall from their grasp. Slowly, one step at a time they made their way up the steep steps until they reached the top safely. The enormous oak doors leading into the temple were wide open and guards stood each side of the doors with heads bowed and the silence was the silence of finality as the crowd watched the funeral party disappear into the temple out of sight.

The temperature was cooler away from the day's heat, hundreds of candles had been lit and the unmistakable acrid tang of burning sage filled the air. Inna was glad to be free of the crowd. She could see in the centre ahead of her the hole in the ground where Alannis was to be placed; suddenly her heart began to thud within her chest. She removed her shoes, as they were forbidden to be worn in this part of the temple, the coldness of the tiles sent a shiver up her spine. The funeral party was now entering the most sacred part of the temple the floor was covered in marble tiles painted in geometric shapes and symbols all layered out within a large circle. Today a few of the tiles had been removed and a burial place made ready. This area of the temple was only normally open to the high priests who perform ceremonies and rituals. They believe their powers are enhanced because the Keepers of the Stone are all buried beneath the ground. Many report that when they work in this area they feel strong surges of energy rise up through their feet and can feel energised for days after spending time here.

Gently the six men begin to lower the small casket into the ground, Inna watches in silence as a worm falls immediately onto the coffin, suddenly feeling nauseas she turns to Zelda who silently has tears falling down her face, then to Hiliron who's mind seems to be in a far off place. He was certainly going to miss Alannis as much as she was, then her thoughts are shaken by the sound of dirt falling onto her Grandmothers casket, a terrible haunting sound of finality. There was no more denying death

A sharp pain attacked her chest she struggled for breath then finally the tears came gushing out uncontrollably. The realisation that her Grandmother would no longer be there for her to run to each day, or to talk to, or laugh with, was more than she could bear, and she began to shake hysterically, and she felt her heart would break. Hiliron and Zelda shocked and concerned for Inna forgot their own grief and turned immediately to console her, she, who had been so brave, so strong, had found her moment to let go. For the longest time they stood with their arms around her allowing her the time to shed her grief. For a long time the only sound to be heard was that of weeping.

Hiliron and Zelda had taken Inna back to the living quarters and Zelda had gently led Inna to her bed, soothing her head encouraging her to fall asleep which did not take long as the day's events had exhausted her. She continued sobbing while she lay sleeping. Zelda watched concerned for some time. There was a knock on the door and Teka appeared.

'Father has sent me with a potion for Inna.'

He looked over at Inna, concern showing on his young face, Zelda waved him over to them. Teka gently held Inna's hand, he loved her so much it broke his heart to see her so upset. Zelda gently shook Inna.

'Inna my dear, Teka has brought you a potion. Drink this, my dear, it will help you sleep more restfully.'

Half dazed, Inna drank the potion, she noticed Teka and squeezed his hand acknowledging his presence then she lay back onto her pillow and quickly fell into a deep, peaceful sleep.

CHAPTER FIVE

A loud knock awoke Hiliron from his sleep, struggling to open his eyes, he could still see the image of Alannis and was reluctant to leave her. Agitated and awake now he threw the bedclothes away from him.

'All right, all right.... I am coming.' Lifting the latch on the door he opened it to a bemused young guard.

'Well, what is it, what do you want?'

'Sir... Calem the Transporter is here and he is insisting on seeing Inna immediately.'

'Well he can wait.'

'Ahem.'

'Well?'

'He says it's a matter of life and death sir.'

'Oh, very well, I'll come right away then.'

'Sir'

'Yes? What is it man?'

'Don't you think you should put some clothes on first?'

Hiliron looked down at himself.

‘Ah........ Good point. Inform him I shall be with him directly.’

‘Sir, there is something else you should know, he is really angry and he is threatening to search the palace for Inna.’

‘Oh is he indeed, well we will see about that.’

Hiliron was greeted by a very grim faced Calem.

‘About time, why isn't Inna with you?’

‘And a good morning to you too,’ Hiliron had no intention of being bulldozed by anyone, least of all Calem.

‘Cut the crap, where is she?’

‘Sleeping.’

‘Does she not understand the seriousness of this situation?’

These two men were like two bulls squaring up to each other, both were used to getting their own way and both were used to issuing orders, neither one liked being spoken to in a subservient way.

‘Perhaps it is you who do not fully understand exactly what has happened here. Let me just enlighten you.’ Calem’s pushiness was now starting to get on Hiliron's nerves.

‘Firstly, Inna is only fifteen years of age, she has just lost her only living relative, not only has she just become Queen of Lithmore but she has the added responsibility of being the Keeper of the Stone.’

‘But she is not taking responsibly for the stone is she?’ snapped Calem. ‘And she promised me she would help.’

‘I am afraid she became so overcome by the last few day’s events, that we had to sedate her last night, and that dear sir is why she did not attend you.’

The furrow marks in Calem's forehead deepened.

‘We have a child close to death.’

The grim fear on Calem's face shouted out. Damn, thought Hiliron, we have been so wrapped up in our own grieving. This is a desperate man. He turned towards one of the guards and instructed him to raise Inna immediately. Calem released a sigh of relief. Hiliron outstretched his hand to touch Calem's shoulder.

‘Forgive us; we are not ourselves at the moment. ...... These are difficult times.’

Calem nodded his head.

‘I suspect that is true for all of us,’ he agreed.

Hiliron was the first to see Calem's magical powers of transportation because as soon as he had instructed him to bring his sick to the palace he vanished and within moments returned with a small boy in his arms.

‘This is my sister’s boy.’

The child lay limp in Calem’s arms, looking pale in colour with oozing sores all over his tiny body. Hiliron grimaced realising that they must act quickly if they were to save him. Alannis would have been horrified if she were here, he shook his head in shame.

Inna too was keenly aware that she had neglected her duties to the Living Stone. Having been alerted, she was now dashing frantically to the great hall, guilt and panic racing through her veins. She chastised herself for not attending to Calem sooner, praying that her disregard would not result in anyone's death. Her fears mounted when she arrived in the great hall.

‘I am so sorry.’ Looking at the small child she knew they had very little time.

'Come we must go,' without saying another word she turned and began to walk quickly across the hall towards the home of the Living Stone.

Within minutes they arrived outside the door of the chamber. Calem was unsure what was about to happen, he had heard many stories about the magical power of the Living Stone, how it was able to heal and bring people back from the brink of death. He looked down at his young nephew and hoped all those stories were true for his sake. Inna entered the chamber first, followed by an unusually nervous Calem but surprisingly as soon as he entered the room he felt a deep warm sensation penetrate through his body. Inna led them to the centre of the room where the stone dwelt, feeling somewhat anxious she offered a silent prayer that all would be well but looking at the child, her fears were not alleviated at all. We cannot fail, we must not fail, she said to herself.

She took the child from Calem and placed him onto the stone then took one step back. For a moment everything appeared still and peaceful, then Calem's eyes widened in disbelief, he felt sure he was seeing the stone move. That's not possible, he thought blinking his eyes, he checked again and sure enough the stone had become fluid rather than solid, bright dazzling colours radiated throughout the chamber, radiant white sparks erupted from the stone. The sound of singing began. Turning his attention to the voice Calem was flabbergasted to see Inna several feet above him looking iridescent. Was he dreaming? Every cell in his body began to tingle with a most pleasurable sensation, what joy what bliss he was feeling, this was wonderful.

The singing stopped and the swirling colours diminished, the chamber silent once more with just the flickering of the candles and an enormous sense of peace. Calem looked down at the boy, his eyes still closed he did not move, concerned Calem brushed a strand of hair from the boy's forehead.

'Were we too late?'

Calem felt nausea. Inna stared at the boy unsure; she had expected the child to be ok.

'I don't know.'

Please, please, please dear child come back to us, she screwed her eyes so tight to make her plea she did not see the boy stir.

'Look, ...look Inna!'

The young boy began to rub his eyes as though to clear them, and then eagerly began to inspect his arms and legs. A broad smile began to light up his face as he gazed up at a very relieved uncle.

'I am better, uncle Calem, look see,' he pointed to were the sores had been.

Calem scooped the young boy up into his arms and swung him around. The child squealed with delight. For the first time Calem revealed his perfect white teeth and broad smile. How handsome, thought Inna.

Overjoyed at the little boy's recovery, Inna was keenly aware that there were many others that needed the stone's healing, so the rest of the day was spent with Calem bringing all of his sick people to the chamber, one by one Inna would lead them to the stone. Inna did not sing, there was no need, the stone pumped out its healing energy to each recipient, all they needed to do was lay their hand upon the stone for a brief moment. Calem observed their faces as each person came out of the chamber completely healed with broad grins on their faces and, for a rare moment, Calem felt humbled.

'We did it, we have finished.'

'Well done, Inna, I don't quite know how to thank you.'

'No thanks required, um ...... but there is something you can do for me.'

'What would that be?'

'Well not to be rude or anything, but you could do with a wash.'

'Ouch,'

Calem looked surprised; he had never had anyone ask him to bathe before. He sniffed his armpits and immediately pulled a face.

'I see what you mean. It's been a rough week. It shall be done,' and with an impish glint in his eye he vanished from Inna's sight leaving her looking around the chamber for him.

'What do you think?' not a minute had past and Calem was back in the chamber standing in front of Inna.

'How do you do that?' then looking at the freshly washed Calem, Inna was even more amazed.

'But you have only been gone seconds, how do you do that?'

'Transporters like me are able to travel anywhere, into any time. You think I have only been gone for a few seconds but for me I have been gone for several hours.'

'Wow that is some gift you have there.' Inna thought for a moment.

'You know with all gifts comes responsibility.'

'Um, you don't say.' the pair of them burst out laughing.

'Hungry?'

'Famished.'

'Then I think it is time we go and find some food.'

The darkness that Calem had brought with him on that first day seemed a distant memory as time went by. He remained at Lithmore for several weeks before returning back to his homeland with his people. They had decided to return home by foot as they were travellers by nature and were eager to explore new territory on the way. Surprisingly, a strong friendship had developed between himself and Hiliron. Teka, although a little jealous of Calem, was in awe of him. Knowing Calem to be a great warrior, he was eager to learn as much as he could from him and even Zelda, who had been distant with Calem, had begun to warm to him and had occasionally been seen flirting with him. Inna was delighted; in many ways having Calem around had made it easier for her to adjust to all her new duties. The lovely thing about their new friendship with Calem was he could visit whenever he wanted as often as he wanted and this gave Inna reassurance.

Thinking back to that first day Inna was feeling rather pleased with herself, her first task as Keeper of the Stone had been enormous but she had succeeded and all the fears and apprehension she had experienced now seemed to fade into nothingness and as she lazed under one of the glorious willow trees in the enchanted gardens she could not help but wonder what it was that ordained her, not a child but still not yet a full grown women, to be not only the guardian of the Living Stone but also the Queen of her beloved Lithmore and for the first time since these titles had been thrust upon her, she let out a gentle sigh and was at total peace with the duties assigned her. Secure in the knowledge that she was surrounded by good friends and people who loved her.

CHAPTER SIX

Delphine, once a picture of loveliness, sat in the shadows of the great hall. Dressed, as she always did these days, in dark clothes wearing a black cape with a large hood so big it almost covered her face. Her sad grey eyes moved around the vast hall taking in all the magnificent furnishings.

A high ceiling painted with a nocturnal sky, splattered with stars, was supported by large columns. The surrounding walls were covered with decorative pictures, rich vibrant colours reached out to you. How sad, thought Delphine, that a place of so much beauty should reek of such fear. The energy felt so heavy, it almost took her breath away. She fixed her gaze upon the cause of this luridness and wondered how a creature of such beauty could be so evil and rotten. Her eyes had rested upon her daughter who was sitting at the head of the hall perched upon her appointed throne, smiling so sweetly and angelically, she looked no more than a child, a small petite little thing with hair as white as snow, her skin fair with just a hint of rose to her cheeks and lips, her eyes large and bright, the colour of lavender, so beautiful and captivating yet so vile.

Cynthiana had been a longed for child. Both the King and Delphine had waited many years for a succession to the throne but to no avail, it seemed it was not to be, then one day a female dwarf named Miska arrived into the tranquil Kingdom of Maro. At first Miska appeared very sweet and charming, not at all like her kind who were usually rude and obnoxious. She seemed eager to please and when she had learnt that the King and Queen longed for a child she quickly made herself known stating that she had magical powers and that a potion could be made that would ensure an heir would be forthcoming.

Within months of receiving the potion and a combination of nature the Queen gave birth to a baby girl. The royal household was thrilled and for a few years everything was well and the King and Queen delighted in their beautiful daughter. They had been so pleased with Miska that they would have been willing to grant her anything, so when she asked that she be allowed to be the child's nanny the King and Queen had agreed without hesitation. This had been a big mistake.

Despicable little creature, thought Delphine as she watched Miska sitting like a lap dog at the foot of Cynthiana. Had Delphine known the result of her bearing a child she would rather have remained barren than responsible for bringing this evil horrid mortal into being. Miska had tricked both she and her husband into believing that their child would be a joy to them both, when all along she had only been the vessel to carry the child Miska wanted to bring into the world, she didn't even look like them. Cynthiana bore no trace of her parent's genes and, as for magic, Delphine and the King had been simple kind people, there had been no need for magic in their lives, yet Cynthiana was full of it and what she had not been born with Miska had taught her through the years.

The odd thing about Miska was, that although for many years she led Cynthiana, as time went by Cynthiana's powers became stronger and more sophisticated, she then became the more dominant and Miska the follower, it was almost as if Miska had created her own mistress yet she seemed comfortable in this role continuing to adore Cynthiana and willing to serve her every need. Delphine knew in her heart that the pair of them were responsible for the King's death, In their eagerness to seize the throne. Of course it had been subtle, she had no proof and even if she could prove it, what good would it do, it would probably result in her losing her own life, although sometimes she wondered if she would not be better off dead. Just then her thoughts were interrupted by the portal doors on the west side of the hall swinging open, a shot of light burst into the centre of the vast space. Delphine shifted uncomfortably in her chair knowing that travellers through the west door never visited with a successful end.

‘Start the music,’ instructed Cynthiana cheerfully.

‘Let them have music to walk to,’

and so the music began. From the entrance of the portal several men were being pushed and shoved by tall giant men towards the front of the central hall where Cynthiana and Miska sat waiting.

The young Queen got up and rushed towards the frightened looking men, smiling, she grabbed one and kissed his cheek as if he were a long lost brother.

‘Welcome, welcome,’

Cynthiana called out, her smile so sweet and innocent you could be forgiven for believing she was a gentle creature, however, the men before her knew different, her smiles were just a precursor to throw you off your guard. For a moment the hall fell silent,

Cynthiana stood staring at the terrified men. The smell of fear filled the hall.

‘Right,.... now, down to business I think, Miska, who is first?’

Miska scanned the book that she held in her little fat hands then placed her stubby little finger onto the page and read out the name of Ezra Massri.

‘Ah, Ezra Massri, step forward dear man,’ her sweet voice commanding him to obey.

‘Miska would you be so kind as to read the offence.’ she continued in the same sweet voice.

Miska read out Ezra's offence.

'Ezra Massri you are accused of not producing the required milk tithe to the crown. What have you to say for yourself?'

Ezra, a middle aged man, was looking pale and frightened, beads of sweat began to pour down his face as he prepared to answer.

'We have had a bad drought this year, Your Majesty, the cows have suffered for it, and consequently have not produced the normal amount of milk........... I know it will be better next year,' he added.

'How awful for you.' Cynthiana shook her head sympathetically.

'However,' she went on.

'That does not solve the problem that you cheated us out of our share, and as you can see this is a big palace, lots of people, we need all the milk we can get.'

Cynthiana released a sigh. Poor Ezra began to shake.

'Well what are we going to do with you, Ezra Massri?'

'Kill him, ' Miska snorted.

Ezra gave a sharp intake of breath and froze like a statue not daring to breathe, sweat fell off him like a waterfall.

'Well a lot of good that will do, Miska.' retorted Cynthiana.

'Kill Ezra? Who will tend the cows? No we must think of something else.'

Miska sneered disappointedly, she didn't even like milk, cheese or butter for that matter well not much anyway, not enough to save him.

Delphine clasped her hands together praying the punishment would not be too severe.

'Tell me Ezra how many children do you have?' continued Cynthiana.

'I have eight.'

Oh no not the children, thought Delphine, please don't harm the innocent children.

'Oh that's far too many, no wonder we don't have enough milk.'

Then, as if a bright idea hit her, she announced.

'I have a solution. You will bring the four oldest ones to the palace and they will be put to work here.'

Happy with her solution she kissed Ezra on the cheek. Miska let out an audible grunt. Delphine could not believe her ears. Ezra had escaped with his life and the children would be safe, a small sigh of relief past her lips.

'Go now; I never want to see you here again.' She spun around facing Miska who had a face like thunder but Cynthiana chose to ignore her and continue with her business.

'Right who's next?'

'Zahur Ka,' Miska sulkily called from her little book.

'And what is his crime?'

'He stole from the palace kitchens.'

'Oh dear Zahur we don't discuss punishment for thieves,' she smiled.

'Would you mind terribly standing just there for me.'

Blindly obeying, Zahur moved to the spot Cynthiana pointed to.

‘Ok,’ she said, ‘It's good night for you,’ and pointing a finger at him she mumbled a few words that no one understood then suddenly a dark cloud rose up from the ground, horrible deep guttural noises could be heard, Zahur’s screams rang out around the hall, and then he was gone.

Delphine folded her arms in an attempt to comfort herself, she was feeling sick and terrified both at the same time, but it was not over. Name after name that was called, received the same fate as Zahur, all had very small crimes or had stolen because their families were starving and needed food. Most were good decent people who Delphine had known. She buried her face in her hands and silently wept.

*****

‘You can't go on like this Cynthiana,’ cried Delphine, She was now alone with the young Queen in her private quarters.

‘These are good decent people. Our people. We should be caring for them and you seem determined on wiping them out. It has to stop.’

Delphine was angry with herself for not standing up for her people before now, allowing the fear that she may meet the same fate as those poor men if she stepped out of line, but today's events had been too much, it had to stop. Cynthiana appeared complacent as she lazed on a chair playing with her hair. Delphine waited for a response but there was none only that Cynthiana began humming to herself, it was as if Delphine wasn't even in the room. Staring in disbelief, what kind of monster is she, thought Delphine, the palms of her hands began to sweat.

‘Cynthiana! Please respond to me.’

The young Queen ceased humming and glared at her mother, a look of irritation fired across her face.

‘Look here old women,’ her words full of venom.

‘You no longer have any say, I am your sovereign, you are no more to me than those sapless morons who met their deaths this morning. Don't presume that you have the right to tell me what I should or should not be doing.’

‘But Cynthiana, it is not right.’ Delphine's voice contained fear but it had to be said.

‘Right, ... I decide what is right and don't you forget it.’

Silence fell for a moment then Cynthiana's face transformed back to her usual smarmy self.

‘Let's not fight.’

And with that Cynthiana changed the subject.

‘Have you heard Alannis is dead, that means that grandaughter of hers will not only be Queen but also Keeper of the Living Stone. She is very young don't you think for such a big responsibility?’ Delphine noticed a glint of mischief in Cynthiana's eyes and wondered what on earth she could be thinking but, in true Cynthiana fashion, she laid her plans out to bear.

‘I think the time may be right to take possession of the Living Stone.’

Wide eyed, Delphine could feel her body tense.

‘What could you possibly want with the Living Stone, you know it is sacred. It's wrong, a thought best forgotten.’

Cynthiana smiled and a chill ran up Delphine's spine.

‘Oh I don't just want the stone mother, ... I want Lithmore.’

Delphine tried to hide the terror she was feeling, what on earth was her daughter thinking. Was it not bad enough she ruled Maro she wanted to rule Lithmore as well. Why? But she dare not ask why.

Later that day, Miska moved as fast as she could waddle to reach Cynthiana's chambers full of news that strangers were camping on the outskirts of town.

'There's a whole army of them!' Miska exclaimed, her eyes as big as saucers. 'Men, women, and children.'

'Where have they come from?' asked Cynthiana, trying not to sound in the least bit interested.

'Ryan says it is Calem the Transporter and his people returning home from their trip to Lithmore.'

'Calem! Lithmore!'

Cynthiana immediately rose from her chair and began to pace the floor. Surely fate was shining on her. She had never met Calem the Transporter but she knew of him and his talent for being able to transport himself and anything he touched to anywhere. Cynthiana had an idea.

'Miska, send Ryan to invite Calem here this evening, we shall have a banquet. Inform cook what is happening, if she starts complaining let her know she has four new helpers coming later today, they can help her. Now go.'

The trouble with dwarfs is they are not really designed to go anywhere in a hurry, their feet are too big, and most dwarfs enjoy a large waistline, they find themselves when in a hurry that their head goes first and the body follows. It's quite a funny sight really as they also have large bottoms which follow, thus causing the waddle. Poor Miska is further disadvantaged by her long dress, having to hoist it up, but being the determined creature she is, nothing deters her and in no time she is back in the chamber with Cynthiana, breathless but excited with news. She collapses onto the nearest chair.

'Well, is everything arranged, what did you find out?'

Miska raised her little fat hand.

'Slow down Malady, allow me my breath and all will be revealed.

'I'll take your breath away from you permanently if you don't get on with it.'

Cynthiana was in no mood to be patient; however unlike everyone else in their world, Miska was not afraid of her Queen, for the most part anyway.

'Oh dear, who is in a mood then?' teased Miska.

Cynthiana stomped on Miska's foot.

'Ow that hurt. All right, all right. The gen is this. Calem took a large group of his people to Lithmore to see Alannis, his people were seriously ill with an unexplained illness and needed the power of the Living Stone, but of course when they arrived Alannis was dead and Inna was the new Keeper of the Stone. But apparently the young Inna coped and all is well, so they are now on their way home.'

She also discovered that the Living Stone had more than just healing powers, it also attracted great wealth as grateful recipients of its power gave valuable gifts to its Keeper, and many people went to Lithmore to trade just so they could visit the stone.

'Just as I thought, without the Living Stone, Lithmore would be nothing, there would be no reason for people to go there or trade there. Quick Miska get the maps, if the mines finally reveal themselves to us it will prove the signs are right for us to begin our quest.'

Miska jumped up from the chair and hastily made her way to a small chest in the room, she tapped on it three times then kicked it once, the lid shot open, she reached inside and pulled out a dusty old scroll. Carefully she began to unfold it revealing a blank piece of parchment paper, then mumbling a few words to herself she took her little fat hand and swept it over the bare blank canvas, as she did so shapes began to form, it was a map showing the province of Lithmorian, in the centre lay the city of Lithmore and surrounding the city were several large crosses. For a moment both women stood staring, eyes wide, almost disbelieving, at last, the gold mines had finally revealed their exact location, this was the sign they had been waiting for.

Miska began to laugh revealing several missing teeth.

'I promised you this day would come and it has, it has.'

At last the mines had revealed themselves, Miska was beside herself with excitement and eager to fulfil her dreams.

'It is time to seize Lithmore then we shall have control over the Lithmorian region and power over the mines.'

'Yes, but first I want to secure the Living Stone into our possession. That way it will make it so much easier to take Lithmore. I believe Calem has been sent to us. We shall use him to help us get the stone.'

The two women were dizzy with excitement.

'We must make plans Miska. Once we have the stone we must think of a way to attract people away from Lithmore. I want Lithmore brought to its knees before we send the army in.

'I have an idea Malady; we can cast a spell onto the small lake of Prespa giving it healing powers. People will flood to Maro to receive its waters and to bathe, without the Living Stone the people will be eager to come to Maro and use the healing waters bringing with them their trade.'

'That's a brilliant idea. Of course, the spell won't last, those sort never do, but what do we care, by then I shall have control over Lithmore.'

'And at long last the mines will be ours.'
Both women started to jump up and down and laugh hysterically.

Kadar had heard enough. Silently he slipped away along the narrow dark passage that was hidden behind Cynthiana's chamber, he was covered from head to toe in pig lard and had to stop himself from slipping. He finally arrived at a small stairway and carefully made his way up the steps to the door ahead of him, gently pushing the door open he could see his Queen resting comfortably in a chair. Curled up sleeping peacefully on her lap, lay her pet cat Snub. Hearing Kadar's arrival, Delphine looked up and took one look at him and burst out laughing.

'Kadar, what have you been up to?'

She placed the cat on the floor and stood with her hands on her hips, she was trying her best not to laugh at him but failing miserably.

'Kadar you look a sight. You have been spying again haven't you?'

'Damn dwarf. If I didn't cover myself in this disgusting stuff she would smell me with that nose of hers.'

Delphine laughed again. She grabbed some cloth and handed it to Kadar who began to wipe some of the grease from his hands and face.

'Well dear friend did you find out anything?'

Delphine was eager to learn what Kadar had risked his life for. He was the only person that she trusted completely he had been her protector when she was Queen and continued after the King had died. To Kadar, Delphine would always be his Queen and to her Kadar was her only true friend. He fixed his gaze on her.

‘It's like we feared I am afraid. There is big trouble ahead and I don't know what we can do to prevent it.’

Kadar went on to tell Delphine all that he had heard and saw, about the map, and how Miska had waved her hand over it to reveal Lithmore and the gold mines that lay in the Lithmorian region. How they planned to take over Lithmore so that they could have control over the mines. How they intended to use Calem to steal the stone. Delphine listened to everything her trusted friend had to say, fear mounting as he spoke each word and when he had finished she finally said.

‘I understand now. I should have known Miska would have been behind this, she must have known about the mines all along. She has been waiting for this day to come. We must try and warn Calem somehow. Perhaps tonight, I can slip the pentacle of warning to him; at least it should put him on his guard.’

Kadar thought this was a good idea. As hard as they tried they could not come up with a better idea.

Cynthiana and Miska were still plotting what was to be done. It was vital that they used Calem to get the stone but how was it to be done, then Cynthiana had an inspiration. She knew Calem would not take the Living Stone just because she told him to, oh no, she knew that much about him. He was a strong willed stubborn man; he was not the type to bend to her will easily, she would need to incorporate other means of getting him to do what she wanted.

‘I have a plan; you must make me a potion.’

A wry expression appeared on Miska's face.

‘Would this be for our forthcoming guest by any chance.’

Both women began to cackle at the mischief they were conjuring up.

*****

Cynthiana entered the great hall already alive with loud music playing and dancers performing. Guests were being welcomed with blossomed fragrant wreaths being placed around their necks.

Groups of people were being led to individual tables set with cups, plates and dishes made from blue faience with blue lotus designs. Sumptuous foods, breads, butter, cheese, fattened fowl and beef filled the tables. Young girls scantily dressed carried trays laden with delicious delicate morsels of food eagerly serving the guests.

Aroma of perfume oils filled the air and somehow caused a delightful effect on the senses in a delightful way. Cynthiana was busily scanning the central hall to see if she could spot Calem. The banquet was well under way yet there was still no sign of him. This displeased her. No one kept her waiting. Already beginning to seethe she spotted a man with unusual blond hair at the end of the hall. In the distance she could see his features looked somewhat rugged but the closer she got the more Cynthiana could see that he was a handsome man. Several people had gathered around him like bees to honey. His identity now confirmed as she watched Ryan place a welcome wreath around his neck. For a moment the two men stood chatting then left the other guests and began to walk towards the young Queen.

Cynthiana had decided before he had even reached her that she disliked him, he walked with such arrogance, I will show him, she thought.

By the time Calem reached her she had managed to mask her dislike of him and forced a sweat innocent smile upon her face.

'Welcome, welcome.'

She was gushing with enthusiasm towards her guest. Calem was immediately struck by her beauty and completely captivated by the colour of her lavender eyes.

'This is most kind of you. We were not expecting such a warm welcome.'

Or any welcome, Calem thought to himself. He did not know much about Cynthiana but he had been warned of her cruelty towards her people, it had not taken him long to find that out, by the reaction of the locals to him when they found out he was attending the festivities they immediately became guarded he sensed they did not trust anyone with connections to their Queen. He couldn't help but wonder if this creature of loveliness had an alternative motive for inviting him to her home.

'Follow me.' Smiling sweetly she waved her hand in the air and began to lead Calem towards the head of the hall.

'Our table is this way.'

She led him through a maze of tables and guests until they reached a table larger than all the others. Miska was already sitting on a long bench stuffing her face with food. She looked up with a half crooked smile and gave a large belch. Calem could not hide his surprise at the sight of her.

'What you staring at?'

She brought her arm up over her face and wiped the grease from her chin.

'You never seen a dwarf before?'

Calem studied her for a moment, then, tilted his head to one side.

'Well no. Actually I have not, forgive me for staring but I was taken aback by your beauty.'

Miska began to snigger, her belly began to wobble like jelly then a roar of laughter came out of her mouth along with some remains of food she was eating.

‘Oh we have a charmer here’ she said, slapping her hand on the table.

‘Sit, eat, drink and enjoy,’

Calem sat himself opposite the repulsive little creature who continued to chuckle under her breath.

‘And who have I the honour of sitting next to?’

Calem had turned to the veiled woman sitting to his right.

‘This is my mother.’

Cynthiana answered for the veiled woman.

‘She does not speak in public, and as you can see she is still in morning for the loss of my dear father.’

Delphine Shifted uncomfortably in her seat. A reaction that did not go unnoticed by Calem. What a strange trio of women thought Calem, a creature of undeniable beauty, an ugly fat dwarf, and a women, well he could not see her, he could not tell if she was young or old or fair of face, the one thing he knew for sure about her was she was not like these other two. He felt a sadness with her, a gentleness about her. What an odd situation he found himself in. What on earth was he doing here.

The evening progressed as did most banquets with the music getting louder, the guests getting drunker, people stuffing themselves to the limit.

The magicians made an appearance and while Cynthiana and Miska's attention were firmly fixed on trying to spot how the magicians did their tricks, Delphine took her opportunity to slip Calem the pentacle of warning, with a quick glance to ensure no one was watching she nudged Calem's knee underneath the table with hers to get his attention. Surprised, Calem looked at the veiled woman whose eyes were instructing him to look down; she quickly pressed the pentacle of warning into his hand. Gazing at it he immediately read its warning, looking up he could see in Delphines eyes that she was pleading with him. Something was wrong here, very wrong, he decided that he would make his excuses and leave but at some point he was going to have to come back to find Delphine, she was in danger, he was sure of it. He rose from his seat to leave and as he did so he began to feel woozy. The last thing he saw was the surprise in Delphine's eyes.

CHAPTER SEVEN

Two beefy men threw Calem's unconscious body onto the cold stone slab. Cynthiana was still heaving from the stench of the human excrement from the nearby dungeons but it did not prevent her from shrieking orders to her guards to get out and ensure that the other prisoners remained quiet. If they failed she was going to personally rip their hearts out. The two young guards left the cell quivering with fear, Miska sniggered, it delighted her that such big strong men were so afraid of her mistress.

The cell was small but quite suitable for what they needed to do, Cynthiana needed to ensure they would not be disturbed and that she was as far away as possible from her mother's prying eyes. Something was going to have to be done with that women, she thought, but for now she was feeling nervous, she had never before attempted to possess another body. She glared down at Calem's lifeless form.

'You've given him too much you old fool he's dead.'

Disgruntled, Miska reached up and placed her head on Calem's chest.

'He is fine, I know what I am doing,' she responded sulkily.

Cynthiana felt slightly guilty for doubting her little companion.

'Of course you do, and I must say, it was a masterpiece to infuse the wreath, who would have thought that the potion would seep into his skin that way. Genius, pure genius.'

Miska puffed up with pride. Yes it had been genius, she thought.

'Well are we ready? Shall we go and show little Inna how the big girls play?'

Cynthiana laughed out loud.

'We're ready Malady.'

For a moment a look of uncertainty flashed across Cynthiana's face.

'Watch over me while I am gone my Miska.' Her words were unusually tender. Miska gave a reassuring smile.

'Ok I am ready.'

She then faced Calem and began to inhale some deep breaths, as she exhaled, black mist poured from her mouth, she continued to take in deep breaths and expel the black mist until she and Calem were completely encompassed by it. Miska watched wide eyed as the mist abruptly vanished taking Cynthiana with it. Alone now in the cold damp dungeon Miska stared at Calem's inanimate body her heart began to race, had something gone wrong, she wondered. Then Calem's eyes shot open and began to search the room, unsure Miska stood back, a broad grin grew upon Calem's face.

'I've done it.' he said.

Still dubious Miska remained guarded.

'It's me, it's me.'

Cynthiana jumped of the slab but Miska remained transfixed, looking back Cynthiana gave a sharp intake of breath at the sight of her lifeless body lying on the slab.

‘That's just my body Miska, here I am, we did it, I am now Calem, he still lays sleeping in my body, all's well.’

Relieved Miska cracked a toothless grin.

‘We did it Miska.’

‘Yes, yes,’ Miska excitedly clapped her hands together.

‘Wow, I like this sensation of being tall.’ Cynthiana gave a little chuckle,

‘Well I wouldn't know anything about that, being a dwarf an all, what I do know is, you don't have much time before the magic wears off. ‘

‘Ok bossy boots, I am going.’

‘Ok Calem the Transporter let's see what you are made off.’

Cynthiana felt a strange tingling sensation start in her toes quickly rising up to the top of her head then a pulling as though someone had just grabbed her feet then nothingness.

She wasn't sure where she was as she lay on the cold floor looking up at the ceiling of the chamber, dazed she shook her head as though to clear it, sitting up to get her bearings she realised she was right behind the Living Stone itself and could reach out and touch it with her hand. The excitement of having successfully transported made her want to get up and do a little jig but just then she heard a humming noise. Someone was in the room with her. Rats, who on earth could that be? she thought. Slowly she got to her knees and peered over the crystal to see a woman in very fine clothes cleaning. What on earth is a woman of her stature doing cleaning? Cynthiana almost let out an audible groan. Think, think, what am I to do? Well one thing was for sure she was not going to let this woman, whoever she was, prevent her from taking the stone. She knew all she had to do was touch it and she and the stone would be gone. That's what she would do, she would be brazen, she would let the woman see her, perhaps she would recognise Calem hopefully and he would get the blame, what could be better and without further thought she stood up and embraced the stone.

Zelda heard a sound behind her and turned around to see what it could be. To her shock and horror she saw Calem stretched out over the Living Stone, he had a strange grin on his face as he stared straight at her, then, there was nothing, he and the stone vanished from the chamber leaving Zelda speechless and bewildered. She immediately fled from the chamber screaming hysterically.

*****

In the enchanted gardens Teka and Inna lay basking in the sun. Teka watched Inna's chest rise and fall with each breath as she lay with her head resting on his belly, he was acutely aware that recently her physical form had developed more womanly curves, he smiled to himself as he soaked in her features her face glistening from the sun with tiny beads of perspiration on her upper lip, how he loved her, a waft of perfume hit his nostrils exciting his senses and he felt a forbidden stirring inside and although he had an uncontrollable urge to pull her to him, to feel her lips upon his, he knew it was not the right time.

Hiliron watched the two youngsters from the terrace, a bemused smile upon his face, he understood Teka’s feelings for the young Inna had matured but he knew that Teka must be patient, Inna was younger than him and was still not quite fully grown although of late she certainly was looking like a young women. There will be plenty of time for their love to blossom, thought Hiliron. One day, in the not too distant future, Inna will wake up and see Teka not just as her childhood friend but her heart will begin to flutter, she will have an urgency to be with him, and love will open its doors to her. Their unity is sure to happen as certain as the sun rising in the morning, they have always been destined for each other,

Hiliron was sure of this. Their souls belonged to one another and Hiliron was glad, Teka had been a lovely child and was developing into a good and trusted man. Hiliron felt assured that, when he was no longer able to protect Inna, Teka would take his place.

Suddenly Hiliron's thoughts were interrupted, the door burst open and a flushed Zelda came scurrying into the room with her headdress askew, tears streaming down her face. She was quickly followed by several of the temple guides looking just as flustered. With raised eyebrows Hiliron looked upon the ensemble of people gathered in his room.

'What on earth is the matter my dear?' asked a very confused Hiliron.

Crying uncontrollably Zelda was unable to speak.

'It is the stone sir,' said one of the guards, his eyes as big as saucers, his mouth open in disbelief as he continued.

'It's gone!'

Zelda threw her hands in the air and cried louder. In an attempt to try and calm her Hiliron took her by the hands and led her to a nearby chair.

'Sit my dear, calm yourself.' He gently pressed her into the chair.

'It is impossible for the stone to vanish there must be some mistake.'

'No, no,' shrieked Zelda.

'There is no mistake I saw the whole thing.'

She began to wail even louder. The woman is hysterical, thought Hiliron and realising something must be done ordered one of the guards to fetch Abron, who was Lithmore's leading medicine man and who also happened to be Teka's father. Hiliron was confident that he would be able to give her something to calm her. Meanwhile he patted her hand reassuringly.

As soon as Abron arrived Hiliron ordered Belja the chief guard to follow him out of the room. Hiliron was relieved to be walking down the corridor away from Zelda's loud wailing sounds, although he felt sorry for her; he was never very good with crying women. For a man of so many years it was surprising the speed at which Hiliron walked. Belja a fit and much younger man found himself almost running beside him.

Within minutes they arrived at the living chamber, immediately they sensed a change in the room, the energy felt flat and uninviting,

a nothingness. The space empty where the Living Stone should be. How can this be, he thought. It's impossible, the outer chamber is always guarded and besides the weight of the stone would present problems to whoever wanted to move it.

Mystified he ordered Belja to scan the room, to look for any clues that could enlighten them to what had happened to the stone. After some time both men were more confused than when they had first entered the chamber, there were no clues whatsoever to be found.

Having seen enough they arrived back to Hiliron's room to find Zelda much calmer, she sat sipping a green liquid that Abron had given her and it seemed to be doing the trick. Hiliron crossed the room to sit opposite her. He studied her for a moment wondering what it was she had seen.

'Now my dear, are you up to telling me what it is you saw?'

His face was kind and encouraging, Zelda smiled weakly.

'Now it's important that you tell us everything. Can you do that for me?'

Zelda shook her head, inhaled deeply then straightened her back as she began to recall the cause of her distress.

'As you know, Inna has given me permission to take flowers into the chamber each day, it is a little something I thought I could do that would please the stone and to keep the area clean; Inna trusted me and I felt honoured to do it. As you know, no one is allowed in the chamber unless they are receiving healing so it is always a great privilege and joy for me to be allowed in there. Well this morning began like any other. I arose early and went out into the garden to gather the fresh flowers, when I arrived at the door of the living chamber the guards stood one each side of the door as normal.'

'Who were the guards?' Hiliron interrupted.

'Miko and Teller,' she replied.

'Um, two very trustworthy men,' commented Hiliron.

'We will talk to them later. Please go on Zelda.'

'As I entered the chamber all appeared and felt normal. I was replacing the flowers with the fresh ones, then when I was finishing my flower arrangement my back was towards the Living Stone. I heard a noise, I suddenly felt the hairs on the back of my neck raise up and I became very cold, I turned towards the stone and there,...... and there,' Zelda began to splutter and cry again.

'Please try and go on Zelda.' Hiliron was eager to hear what it was she had seen.

'Standing in front of the stone,' she spluttered.

'Was,' she sniffled again.

'Was..... Calem.'

'Calem,' Both Hiliron and Abron echoed in unison.

'What on earth was he doing there?' Hiliron spoke more to himself than was asking a question.

'He just stared at me,' Zelda continued.

'As if he did not know who I was and then he laid onto the stone, looked up at me and smirked, I felt fear right through to my bones. Then all of a sudden there was a colossal flash of light, inside my head I heard an awful scream, I covered my face I thought surely I was going to die, then it was silent and cold in the chamber. I opened my eyes and Calem and the stone had vanished.'

Zelda began to cry again but this time it was quieter a more gentle weeping.

'How could he?' she said, more to herself than to anyone in the room.

'I thought he was our friend, I thought he was my friend. Why has he done this terrible thing?'

The tears rolled down her face now and she made no attempt to hide them. Hiliron patted her hand in an effort to comfort her. This is all very odd, thought Hiliron. Calem was their friend and ally this he was sure of and this was not the action of a friend. Surely Calem had not been acting all this time. He knew, of course, of the friendship between Zelda and Calem, that had not gone unnoticed how they looked at each other, thinking no one knew of their growing romance. Surely that could not have all been an act. Hiliron was also confused that Calem had looked at her as though he had never seen her before, surely he would have shown some recognition in his eyes when he had seen her. It was all very strange concluded Hiliron.

The only thing that did make sense to Hiliron was that the stone could only have been removed by someone with Calem's powers.

'This is terrible!' Hiliron spoke out loud.

Then, as if remembering something, stared at Abron, then rose quickly and rushed towards the terrace, his attention drawn to where Teka and Inna had been. He could see Teka kneeling beside Inna his heart began to beat fast as panic raised within him.

Moving as fast as he could, with Abron at his heals, they raced down the steps and across the yard heading towards the gardens, all the time both of them praying that Inna would be ok, but the closer they got they could clearly see Inna's lifeless body laying on the ground, her face colourless, Teka was nervously hovering over her looking drawn and gravely concerned. Hiliron knelt down taking her hand and began calling her name, she looked so ashen, so young, so vulnerable, Hiliron swallowed hard, and again, he called her name gently at first then panic took over and he became louder and more forceful shaking her limp body. Slowly her eyes began to move behind her closed eyelids.

'Here, place this onto her lips.'

Abron handed Hiliron a vile of liquid, he gently took it from him and placed it on Inna's mouth trying to force her lips apart, the liquid seeped into her body. Slowly, she began to stir, her eyes gradually opening. Glancing around she could see the anxious faces of the three men, and bravely forced a smile.

Hiliron turned to Abron.

'Is she going to be alright?' There was no mistaking the fear in his voice.

Abron pulled Hiliron away from Inna's side.

'Teka says she was perfectly okay when all of a sudden it appeared she was struck by some pain, apparently she had been laying on the ground and had rouse with such a jerk, Teka says she made a ghastly sound as if something was being wrenched from within her.'

Both men looked at each other knowing what that wrenching

sensation was.

'Of course this had all happened at the same time the stone was taken, and we both know what that means,' continued Hiliron,

'I am afraid we do,' agreed Abron.

'This is a great concern Hiliron, as only you and I know the Living Stone and Inna's life force rely on each other for their survival, it is not just what Inna gives to the stone by singing to it daily but what the stone gives back to her, I am concerned if they are parted for too long they will both be lost to us.'

'Don't, Abron, don't even say such things we must get the stone back we must do whatever it takes.'

Both turned to look at the two youngsters on the ground, Teka was tenderly embracing Inna in his arms she was quite alert now and the colour had seeped back into her face. She was smiling up at Teka comforted by his closeness. Teka wanted to say are you all right my darling but all he managed to say was,

'It will be ok, you're feeling better now.'

His heart was raging inside his chest, he had never felt such fear, for a brief moment he thought he was going to lose his beloved Inna and he felt helpless to assist her in any way. He felt angry because he was unable to make everything ok, but relief that whatever it was that had happened to her had passed and she was ok now. He found himself gently rocking Inna back and forth like a baby, as much for his own comfort as for hers.

Inna was taken back to her chamber and put to bed. The elixir Abron had given her had made her very weary and sleep came easy.

Hiliron, as chief advisor to the throne, and Abron, who was Lithmore's master healer and counsellor, knew things that others did not, they talked in secret for many hours and decided that no one at the moment should know that not only was the stone's existence in danger but also Inna's life . They discussed at length the importance of getting the stone back, possible ways of going about it, and what steps they should take to help Inna. Abron knew of a few potions that would sustain her for a while but time was of the essence in getting the stone back to its rightful place. Hiliron and Abron were clever men and with the evidence they had gathered certain things did not make sense. Of course they believed Zelda when she said it was Calem she had seen in the chamber but something was just not right. Hiliron felt it in his guts, in his bones and in his heart.

CHAPTER EIGHT

Delphine had been horrified as she had helplessly watched Calem slump to the floor. Two guards had rushed past her, pushing her to one side, then roughly dragging the unconscious Calem away. The great hall continued to be alive with music and dancing and the guests seemed oblivious to the events that surrounded them or perhaps they were too drunk to care.

Delphine had tried to follow the guards to see where they were taking poor Calem only to be stopped by Cynthiana, who had disregarded the fact that Delphine was her mother and had thrown her hard against the wall in such a fury, pinning her forearm across Delphine's throat and threatening her to mind her own business.

'Nothing,' she had said,

was going to stand in her way of getting possession of the Living Stone.

'Even if that means silencing you old woman.'

She had spoken with such venom. Delphine knew in that moment, that even though they were of the same blood, Cynthiana would not hesitate to have her killed. If she was going to survive she was going to have to flee Maro and as soon as possible. How her heart ached for what used to be when her world was full of peace and tranquillity, where everyone was allowed to go about their business and make an honest living, where no one lived in fear, but those days were gone now. There had been a time she could protect her people but now she was no longer Queen, all her authority was lost and she was powerless to stop Cynthiana's senseless killings. Yes the decision was made, she would get as far away from Maro as possible then perhaps there might be a chance she could find a way of stopping Cynthiana and helping her people. It's possible she thought, anything is possible.

Kadar and Delphine waited until late into the night before attempting their escape, they managed to creep past the guards unseen, and walked as fast as the darkness would allow them across the fields that adjoined Maro towards the safety of the nearby forest. Surrounded by trees it was impossible to see a foot in front of them but Kadar insisted that no torch be lit in case they should be spotted.

Delphine had felt her heart race as she constantly stumbled over the uneven ground but Kadar's firm grip on her hand reassured her as they bumbled their way forward going deeper into the forest. How long they had before Cynthiana discovered their escape she did not know, and feelings of guilt mixed in with fear began to overwhelm her at not being able to help Calem, who, she was sure would be dead by now. Cynthiana would use him, then, having no more use for him, she would kill him for sure. She remembered the shock on the young man's face as he collapsed to the ground and the horrible smirk on Cynthiana's face as her henchmen carried him away in the pretence he was in a drunken stupor. She had rushed after them in a feeble attempt to try and reason with her daughter to stop what she was doing, only to be viciously thrown against the wall and almost choked to death by her. It was then that she felt no longer safe, that who she was and who she had been did not count for anything. Cynthiana would, if it suited her, kill her. Tears began to blur her vision and she found it difficult to catch her breath as these thoughts whirled around in her mind.

'Please Kadar, can't we slow down?'

'It's not far now,' was all he had said.

He had been right; a few moments later from out of the shadows appeared a man with two horses. It was old Ty, he had been a guard years ago when she had been Queen, she smiled gently to herself, there were still those brave enough and loyal enough to help her.

'I can't thank you enough Ty for helping us,' her voice full of appreciation.

'But you must promise me, you will be very careful, when you return.'

'Don't you worry about me Your Majesty; I have no intentions of returning to Maro.'

They said their farewells to old Ty and with two horses and enough supplies of food, tools and clothing they continued their journey. Kadar felt it was safe enough now to light a small torch to help guide them through the remaining forest and it was not long before they came to a small stream that led them out into the open landscape. They had mounted their horses and were now able to ride fast under the light of the moon.

They arrived early morning to a quaint little run down dwelling tucked beside a small waterfall close to a copse of trees.

'How delightful,' exclaimed Delphine

'Where are we exactly?'

'We are on Torre Plains tucked away where no one will find us.'

Kadar looked around him he had a look of belonging in his eyes.

'This is where I was born,' he added.

'Really!' A look of surprise shot over her face.

'Really.'

The gentle sound of the waterfall was like music to her ears.

'I love it,' she exclaimed smiling.

Kadar felt pleased; it had been some time since he had seen his lady smile.

They should have both been tired after their long journey, but instead of sleeping they had set to work, cleaning the old dwelling place making it fit for habitation. Kadar gathered wood and very quickly had a fire started. He had also managed to catch some fish and placed them on a spit to cook. Delphine had done her fair share of chores; no one would have guessed she had been a Queen, and by nightfall the little house was fit to sleep in. The smell of their dinner cooking filled the air.

At last they both relaxed contentedly by the lit fire out in the open air admiring their first day's work, chatting about this and that, when Kadar said.

'You know Ma Lady, I am so very sorry, things have turned out the way they have for you. The King would be heartbroken if he could see what has happened, and for all the hopes and dreams you had for young Cynthiana, for her to turn out the way she has must be devastating for you.'

Delphine pondered Kadar's words for a moment, and then said.

'You're right. If the King were alive today and witnessed what was going on, it would have killed him. Oh hold on it did.'

They both gave a ironical laugh.

'Cynthiana has done some terrible things but this latest stunt of hers I feel will be her undoing, or should I say, I hope it will be her undoing. To think that she can possess something as good and sacred as the Living Stone and keep it for her own gain, well it's just not right. When I carried her in my belly I thought I was going to bring a child into this world that would enhance our kingdom not one that would be a greedy and destructive being. I curse the day I ever set eyes on that witch dwarf, Cynthiana belongs to her, not me.'

Delphine sighed. Kadar reached over and gently patted Delphine's hand. Remembering Calem and the fate he surely must have met, Delphine's eyes began to well up.

'I wish we could do something to put things right.'

For a moment they both sat contemplating their own thoughts then Kadar spoke.

'The universe has a way of putting things back into balance, this I truly believe, by clinging to the laws of nature that something good must surely happen soon to address the balance.'

'Yes, of course you are right.' Delphine agreed.

'Let's hope it happens soon,' they both let out a sigh.

'We must have hope my Queen.'

'Don't you think it is about time you called me by my name, after all you are my closet friend in all the world, and I would like it.

Kadar nodded his head gently but thought to himself no matter what he called her she would always be his Queen.

*****

'Calem, Calem, are you ever going to wake up?'

Calem could hear the familiar voice of his sister Nina calling to him. Struggling to open his eyes he felt his body begin to shake as a hand touched his shoulder and began to rock him back and forth, gently at first then with more vigour.

Managing to open his eyes, everything appeared blurry but he could see enough to know he was in a small room with a fire burning in the corner and white sheep skin rugs carpeting the floor. Two chairs sat one each side of the fireplace. As his eyes became less blurry he recognised one of the old chairs as his favourite tatty chair he loved to sit on and immediately he felt comforted. He was home.

Calem stared in disbelief at the figure hovering over his bed; it was indeed his sister Nina. She plunked herself down onto the bed beside him.

'Well, brother, that was a bender and a half.'

'What do you mean?' Calem managed to ask.

'Well, some of our men found you just outside camp, paralytic, you must have wondered off in the middle of the night and passed out, boy did you stink of ale.'

Calem sat up in bed confused, a stabbing pain shooting through his head, he certainly felt as if he had a hangover.

'Here drink this.'

'Ewgh that's disgusting what is it?'

'It's pickled sheep's eyes now get it down you, stop being such a baby. It will do you good.'

Still dazed and confused Calem held his nose and poured the foul mixture down his throat.

'Tell me, where was I when you found me?'

'Well on Torre Plains of course just a day's journey from home.'

‘Torre Plains!’ he exclaimed.

Calem could not remember reaching Torre plains, he could not remember getting drunk, in fact he was finding it hard to recall his last memory and where he was.

‘What's wrong Calem? You look worried?’

‘Something is wrong sis, I feel it in my bones. For a start, as you very well know, I never drink to excess and why would I get drunk on my own? Why can't I remember being at Torre Plains? In fact,’

his face was full of concentration,

‘The last thing I can remember is packing up and leaving Mier Falls.’ Nina looked surprised.

‘That was five days ago.’

They both sat in silence trying to figure out what this all meant. Something was certainly odd about the whole situation.

‘Tell me the events from when you found me at Torre Plains.’

‘Well, everyone arose early morning ready to break camp excited because we all knew by nightfall we would be home finally. You were nowhere to be seen so Lin checked your tent and found it empty. Once we were sure you were not in the camp a search party was sent out to look for you. It did not take them long; they found you about a quarter of a mile from camp completely comatose. We assumed, because you stunk of ale that you were drunk, we put you on a wagon and continued our journey home, and here we are.’

Calem thought for a moment.

‘Right. Move sis, I need to get out of bed.’

He swiftly pushed the blankets away from him and swung his legs over the bed, as he stood up, he felt his legs give way beneath him.

'Woah there, matey boy, me thinks you're trying to move a little too fast.'

She rushed to his side grabbing his arm to support him, giving him long enough to regain his strength.

'Ok, sis I think I am ok now.'

Slowly he made his way to a small table in the corner of the room, a bowl and a jug of water stood waiting upon it. Carefully he poured some of the water from the jug into the bowl and began to wash his face. He was desperate to clear his head and figure out why he could not remember the last few days. As he splashed the cold water on his face he was certain of one thing, he was going to get to the bottom of this. Something was wrong, very wrong, First, he needed to retrace his steps, he decided he would start by returning to Torre Plains.

*****

Cynthiana and Miska had journeyed deep beneath the palace into hidden caves that ran beneath the city of Maro. Milky white stalactites and stalagmites joined together creating huge columns appearing to support the ceilings of the cave. Before them the bright light radiated from the Living Stone illuminating the surrounding pools of water transforming their normally dull colour into a bright translucent turquoise. For a moment they both stood mesmerized staring at the stone.

'We did it Miska.' Both women were feeling extremely pleased with themselves.

'It is very beautiful even if I do say so.' Miska wanted to find fault with the stone but the beautiful colours that radiated from it made it impossible to do so.

'It's a shame Calem managed to escape but it won't matter, he won't remember anything, he and his people won't even remember ever coming to Maro.'

'But I am curious Miska, just before he managed to disappear on us. Why did you drown him in alcohol.'

'I was going to set light to him.'

'Oh, you wicked girl,' both women screeched with laughter.

Their attention was brought back to the Living Stone and for a moment they both stood quietly staring at the swirling colours radiating from it.

'Do you think the stories are true, that the stone is capable of bringing people back from the dead?'

'I don't know Ma Lady. Maybe?'

'Hmm if it were true, think of the power we would have.' Cynthiana sighed contented with her days work.

'Come Miska I am exhausted we must get some rest, we still have Lithmore to conquer then the gold mines are ours and once that is done I shall be the most powerful woman on the earth.'

She began to laugh so loud the sound resonated around the caves echoing. She did not notice that Miska was not smiling with her.

*****

After a ravenous breakfast Calem informed his sister that he was going to return to the place where they had found him on Torre Plains to have a look around to see if he could remember anything. He knew Torre Plains well, his sister described the place where

they had found him and he felt sure he would find it easily.
The sun was shining brightly causing Calem to squint; he had arrived at the place Nina had described to him, however, it seemed the more he searched the more confused he became, nothing seemed to jog his memory. It must be mid day, he thought as the sun was right above him now and the heat was almost unbearable, he remembered that there was a deserted old dwelling close by, with a waterfall besides it. He decided to find it, perhaps after a good swim he would have the chance to think better.

It did not take him long to find the old place but to his surprise it was not deserted, he could see the shape of a female standing by the river, she was dipping a pole into the water, it looked to Calem as if she were fishing. At first she did not hear him. Calem gave a little cough to get her attention the middle aged attractive woman turned to face him. He was eager to assure her he meant no harm but she looked very startled when she saw him. He raised his hands in a gesture to assure her he had come in peace, but her eyes were as big as saucers. For a moment they both stared at each other, until finally the woman spoke.

'Calem,' she exclaimed. 'Calem the Transporter.'

Now it was Calem's turn to look surprised, how did this woman know his name?

'Yes, yes,' he stammered.

'Oh Calem, you don't know how pleased I am to see you.'

Completely confused Calem stood dumbfounded as he watched her throw down her fishing rod and rush towards him.

'Welcome, welcome, I don't know how you found us, I don't care, I am just so glad you have come, let me get you some food and drink.'

Calem was now beginning to believe he was, either dreaming or he was totally losing his mind.

‘Madam, that is most kind of you, but you seem to have an advantage over me, you know my name, but I do not know yours.’

Delphine laughed.

‘Of course you do, I am Delphine we met at the banquet.’

Then she smiled,

‘Of course, you did not see my face. I do apologise, let me introduce myself, my name is Delphine, I am the mother of Cynthiana.’

‘Nope, still not getting it.’ He studied her kind face which by now appeared as confused as he felt. Did this woman hold the key to his missing days.

‘May I take you up on your kind offer of food and drink, and you can tell me how you know me, and I will share with you what I have experienced the last few days then perhaps we will make some sense of all this.’

By now Kader had joined them and they quickly set about retelling each other the past few days events. Things became clearer.

‘So how did we all end up on Torre Plains if we had set up camp outside Maro?’ Calem asked.

‘I can answer that.’ Kadar joined in.

‘Between Cynthiana and that witch dwarf of hers they are more than capable of casting a spell to wipe all memory of Maro from you and your people. I can understand them wiping the memories of your people but what I don't understand is them allowing you to live.’

‘Maybe they did not intend for you to live, maybe you escaped,’ added Delphine.

'I must have because here I am. I don't remember but I guess it doesn't matter now.'

'And we are so glad you are here, safe.' Delphine grabbed Calems hand and squeezed it.

He thought how sweet and gentle she was and how sad it was that her daughter was such a monster.

'Maybe,' she continued,

'The universe is starting to readdress the balance.'

They all smiled, a seed of hope was starting to emerge and Delphine and Kadar knew it was beginning with this young man.

The three talked late into the night. The more they talked Calem began to recall flashes of his forgotten moments. He remembered the great hall and the feeling of someone placing a wreath around his neck, he recalled the loud noise of the drums and in his mind he could see dancers dancing to the music. He remembered Delphine in her black garb with her mask on her face, although the woman that sat with him now looked nothing like her, for now she was wearing a blue robe, her graying hair was exposed and her beautiful face was for all the world to see. Here she was free of her shame. He liked her and Kadar and although he did not know them well he felt a bond of trust between them, a warmth that he had not felt since his parents death.

By morning Calem had decided what he must do. If everything had happened as Delphine had described then the stone would now be missing from Lithmore, and Inna and Hiliron would need his help to get it back. Delphine cooked him a good hearty breakfast and the three talked about his plans to go to Lithmore to help. Both Delphine and Kadar assured him if they could be of any help he knew where to find them, and with that assurance Calem said his goodbyes.

CHAPTER NINE

Calem found himself in the gardens of Lithmore, he had meant to transport directly into Hiliron's quarters but for some reason had miscalculated. Instead he had managed to come face to face with Teka and Inna who stood for a moment with jaws dropped and eyes wide open in disbelief that Calem was actually standing just feet away from them.

‘You!’ Shouted Teka.

And without hesitation, charged with his head down at Calem landing a blow to his stomach, sending poor Calem to the floor with a thud. Before Calem could catch his breath Teka had jumped on top of him and continued to administer punches and demanded to know, in a high pitch voice, the whereabouts of the Living Stone. Regaining his breath Calem managed to push the snarling Teka away from himself.

‘Whoa there, Teka, let me speak, you have it all wrong.’

‘No I don't, you were seen taking it. You are a thief and a liar and we want it back.’

Teka swung at him again but Calem was too fast for him and managed to push him far enough away to allow him enough time to scrabble to his feet. Determined not to give up, Teka charged at Calem once more only to be stopped by Calem's hand against his head. Furiously Teka punched the air in his attempts to strike him.

‘If you would just calm down for one moment I can explain.’

Calem was beginning to lose patience with this young man.

'Stop Teka, he is telling the truth.'

Teka turned to Inna in disbelief.

'I see it, I know it.'

She was holding her crystal for reassurance and, although confused, she knew in her heart, no matter what Zelda had seen, Calem did not take the stone. Teka Stopped.

'Very well. But don't you dare go disappearing on us or anything. You have no idea the trouble you're in.'

Calem gave a wry smile.

'I think, it would be wise if we all went to see Hiliron then perhaps I could tell you all I know.'

'Ok, but no funny business.'

Teka was not fully convinced of Calem's innocence. Calem and Inna raised their eyes at one another. Inna was sure; she had seen into his heart, he was a good man, a man that was here to help them. Teka did not have her gift so he could be forgiven for being more cautious but she felt he was going a little over board now, particularly after she had just told him he was ok, typical, men, they always think they know best, thought Inna.

While on their way to see Hiliron there were a lot of gasps, and ooo's, and whispers behind hands, people stared. One or two people called insults after Calem as they believed he was the one who had stolen the Living Stone. The sooner he was able to clear his name and regain their trust, he thought, the sooner he could set about helping them. Just then a flabbergasted Zelda came running towards them stopping right in front of Calem. For a brief moment a little girl hurt look swept over her face followed quickly by a flash of anger as she raised her hand and brought it down hard on

Calem's face. A sharp intake of breath could be heard from Inna, and a satisfied snort came from Teka.

'How could you?'Zelda screeched.
'How could you do such a thing? Have you any idea of the harm you have done? '

Tears began to well up. She felt betrayed and utterly confused.

'Zelda, please.'

Calem pleaded with Zelda to listen to him, he was saddened by the hurt he saw in Zelda's eyes. The last thing he wanted was for her not to trust him or to think that he could in any way be responsible for this mess.

'You don't know what you have done,' she cried.

As she pounded on his chest with her fists with tears pouring down her cheeks. She had grown very fond of Calem during his time at Lithmore and hated the thought that he had betrayed them, she was feeling particularly vulnerable as she had just learnt from Hiliron the full extent of what the consequence of the loss of the Living Stone meant to Inna and she was beside herself with worry.

'Enough,' came a deep voice from behind the group.

'Calem, would you please come with me.'

Hiliron extended his arm pointing it in the direction of his chamber. Relieved to have an end to Zelda's outburst Calem gave a quick sigh of relief and did as he was asked. Without another word being spoken Hiliron followed directly behind him and closed the door leaving the others standing dumbfounded out in the corridor.

Some time passed, they could hear nothing. Zelda tried putting her ear up against the door but to no avail. Abron appeared; having already been in the chamber, and left returning a short while later with Belja and without speaking to the others, disappeared back into the chamber.

Finally Hiliron appeared at the door and signalled for the remaining three to enter. Teka immediately opened his mouth to speak but saw his father put his hand to his lips so he said nothing. Calem sat relaxed in a chair with his leg hanging over the arm of it. Abron sat at a table with pen in hand and Belja stood by the window deep in thought.

'Ok. This is the situation.' Hiliron, sounded calm and controlled.

'It appears that we now have all the facts. We know how the stone was stolen. We know who has stolen it. We know roughly its whereabouts. Now let me make this clear.'

Hiliron gave a stern look from Teka to Zelda and paused for a moment before continuing.

'Calem was in no way responsible for the taking of the stone.'

Both Teka and Zelda opened their mouths to protest but Hiliron raised his hand.

'Allow me to explain. The rumours we have heard about the new Queen of Maro are true, she is a very devious and dangerous young women, it is believed she murdered her father and now her mother is in exile unable to bear the monstrosities of her daughter. Calem tells us he had the unfortunate misadventure of meeting Queen Cynthiana who, with her accomplice, managed to drug him and by doing so used his body and the gift of transporting to steal our beloved stone.'

'That evil little witch,' spat Zelda.

'But what are we going to do? How are we going to get it back?'

Teka wanted answers and he wanted them now.

'Well first things first,' Hiliron spoke with authority.

'We must declare a council of war.'

A loud thud interrupted Hiliron, everyone's head followed the sound to see that Inna had collapsed in a heap on the floor. Quickly they gathered around the young Queen. Abron rushed to her side and quickly administered to her. Six concerned faces greeted her as she responded to Abron's elixir. A hundred thoughts were racing around her mind but the one question foremost in her head was why? why? was she having these episodes, why was she feeling like her life force was being drained away from her? Calem reached out and lifted her up like she was nothing more than a loaf of bread and placed her on the couch. Teka immediately chastised himself for not thinking quick enough, he should have been the one to take care of her, he went over to the couch to be as close to her as possible, he wanted to glare at Calem to warn him off, but his heart was not in it, Calem was not the bad guy here, in fact he was indeed their friend, he forced a half smile to him, which did not go unnoticed.

'I think,' Inna began slowly,'

'I think,' she paused again, as if she were afraid to put into words what she was thinking.

'I need to know the truth Hiliron. Is my life dependant on being connected to the stone and, if that is the case, are we both dying?'

Her eyes darted from Hiliron to Abron searching their faces for the truth. Their look confirmed her worse fears without them saying a word. Why had her Grandmother not told her of this? For a moment the room fell silent as the severity of the situation dawned on everyone.

Hiliron, sensing the urgency to find a solution, pressed on with his plans.

'I fear this is going to be more complicated than we first thought, but trust me Inna we are not without our powers, we can get the stone back. We have a good strong army of men. Belja will organise them. They can be ready to leave for Maro before nightfall.'

'But they will take days to get there,' Interrupted Teka.

'Why can't Calem just transport himself to the stone and bring it back in the same way Cynthiana took it?'

'Good thinking Teka, but unfortunately Delphine, Cynthiana's mother, assures me Cynthiana will have made sure wherever the stone is, I won't be able to transport with it. She will have secured some anchor on it that won't allow me to just go in and take it, she is too clever for that.'

'So what do we do?' Teka persisted pushing his wild hair out of his eyes in frustration.

Hiliron raised his hand, in a hushing motion.

'Well first of all, we have to determine exactly where the stone is. Calem tells us that Delphine may be able to help us, so I suggest we start with Delphine. You, Calem and Inna must go and speak with her and find out as much information as possible, while we concentrate on the military side of things.'

'Wait a minute,'Zelda cocked her head to one side,

'I'm not staying here. Where Inna goes, I go. You forget Hiliron, I promised her Grandmother I would take care of her and take care of her I shall.'

'Me too.'

Chipped in Teka.

She nodded her head as though she had given her final word on the subject and Hiliron felt it was probably unwise to argue with her and so agreed. With that settled it was decided all four would go to seek Delphine's help.

Abron prepared some more elixirs for when Inna needed them, he knew they would not work many more times, but it was all he had to offer. Zelda rushed off to change into some more suitable clothes for travelling in and when she returned Calem could not help but think she looked like a young girl with her hair tied back in a pony tail, and instead of her long flowing gown, she wore emerald green silk harem pants and a silk top to match. Calem eyed her approvingly.

After assurances that Hiliron and Abron would dispatch an army as quickly as possible to march on Maro, the small group could leave knowing all they had to do was find the stone, and get Inna to it, then lay low until the army reached them, simple. If only it could be that easy unfortunately Calem had grave doubts, but for now he had to keep his concerns to himself, now was a time to be positive and maybe, just maybe, Delphine will know exactly where the stone is.

With everyone ready, they said their goodbyes. Teka Inna and Zelda nervously held hands in a circle with Calem and as their hearts pulsed another beat they were gone from the room. Hiliron and Abron were left staring into an empty space. Hiliron shook his head.

'That's amazing how he does that.'

Abron agreed.

CHAPTER TEN

Who was the more surprised, it is hard to say. The three men hovering over Delphine and Kadar, who were on their knees with their hands tied behind their backs, or the group of Transporters.

Immediately Calem realized that an execution was about to take place, what the hell was he going to do, for one brief moment the executioners stood dumbfounded, confused by the appearance of these intruders, then seemingly gathering their wits, one of the brutes began to charge with his large sword towards the interlopers, quickly followed by the other two. Kadar stuck out his foot managing to trip one of them; he went flying with a thud to the floor. People scattered in all directions trying to avoid their attackers,

Calem pounced in a heartbeat on top of the fallen man, and without hesitation pulled his neck up in a clean break killing him instantly. Zelda and Inna ran towards the trees their hearts racing they could see two of the men chasing towards Teka, but were helpless to aid him. Panic consumed them as they were unarmed against these mad men. Teka was bending down gathering a small rock from the ground he then pulled a catapult from underneath his shirt and quickly loaded it, all the while two furious lethal looking men wielding swords getting closer and closer to him. One tall and agile, the other short and fat. He aimed his catapult at the tall one, ping, the stone went flying through the air with such precision and landed right in the centre of the man's forehead, he immediately collapsed. There was no time for Teka to reload and the second man was now dangerously close to him. Adrenaline rushed through Teka's veins as his attacker lifted the sword high in the air preparing to bring the blade down. Feeling nauseous and with his heart thumping almost as if it would come out of his chest Teka surprised his attacker by leaping forward and head butting him in his large belly, it was enough to make the fat man lose his balance and he and his sword went flying to the ground, for a second he was winded but he was surprisingly agile for such a big man and sprang quickly to his feet grabbing Teka and throwing him across the earth, in an instance he had grabbed his sword.

Teka lay helplessly on the ground the wind knocked out of him, dazed and defenceless he watched helplessly as the fat man held his sword over him. Was this it? Was this to be the day he died? there was no escaping. Beads of sweat fell off his face; his killer was smiling down at him now as he raised his sword up in the air with the intention of driving his blade into Teka's chest. Teka squeezed his eyes closed, he could not bear to look, and there was nothing he could do to save himself. A moment passed, all he could hear was the loud thumping of his heartbeat, nothing happened. He reluctantly opened one eye to see a glazed look upon the man's face.

To Teka's dazed amazement he could see a shiny object protruding out of his attacker stomach, the man’s face was ashen, blood began to pour from his wound. Teka, gathering his senses, immediately rolled out of the way and sprang to his feet. The man was still standing, in a state of shock, it was as if he did not know what to do. Then his knees suddenly gave way and he fell at last to the ground, dead. Calem had been standing behind him. Teka exhaled a loud sigh of relief.

‘Are you ok?’

‘I'm fine,’

Teka began to rub his head and found a large bump.

‘I think I might have a sore head though.’

Teka forced a smile; he had never been so relieved to see Calem.

Zelda and Inna had been watching from a safe distance and came running towards the two men, overjoyed that they were both safe, yet both felt annoyed that they had been useless in helping them. Inna was determined something would have to be done to prepare them better. If they were going to succeed this ordeal each and every one of them would need to have values that would help bring success to retrieving the stone. It was not fair to rely solely on Calem and Teka to protect them. Calem was quick to assure the two women that he felt sure there was going to be ample opportunity along their journey for them to do their part.

‘It's all a matter of knowing one’s own strengths.’ He said,

‘You can't expect to become a warrior, when your whole mind set is all about love and healing, it is unnatural.’

He put his arms around the women, and faced them towards Delphine and Kadar who were still kneeling on the ground with their hands tied behind their backs.

‘Right now I think there are two people who could do with a helping hand.’

He gently pushed them towards the two captives who by now were grinning from ear to ear. Delphine and Kadar had never been so pleased to see anyone in all their lives and now free, they welcomed them with opened arms embracing each one of them as if they had known them for always. Everyone began to talk all at once, questions were asked, who were these men? what were they doing here? Calem felt uneasy he was wary that there may be more men out there and he was keen to dispose of the bodies. They all agreed that they should dispose of the failed executioners as soon as possible. It was decided that Calem and Teka would set to work piling the bodies onto the horses and take them deep into the woods and bury them. They travelled far enough until they found a place suitable then set to work digging a hole just big enough to put the three men in. Then quickly and without ceremony they placed the bodies in the grave and covered it up. Within a few hours the lives of the would be killers were hidden away in the forest forever.

Finally with everyone safe back at camp, there was a chance to talk.

'I am guessing those men were Cynthiana's thugs.' surmised Calem.

'Correct, we thought she might leave us alone, but we think the fact that you escaped made her afraid. The fear of what my knowledge and your powers could do could interfere with her plans and she would never stand for that.'

'So she sent people to murder her own mother.'

Teka's voice was full of disgust and disbelief.

'It was inevitable once she had discovered we had escaped, but also somehow I think she found out we had already spoken to Calem. She has no love for me, her only concern is getting what she wants, and in her mind, we became obstacles that needed to be got rid of and it would have worked if.... '

She broke off and a slight shudder passed through her body at the thought of what almost happened to them.

'But how could she, 'cried Inna.

'How could your own child have you killed, what sort of monster is she?'

Delphine turned to Inna and took her hand. Tears of sadness were falling down Inna's face. Delphine looked into the eyes of this loving compassionate girl and felt her heart would break knowing that she was never destined to have a child with such goodness, she squeezed her hand gently in appreciation of her thoughtfulness.

'But how would she have known you had talked to Calem?'

It was Teka's turn to ask questions.

'Oh that's easy, -I am afraid,- Cynthiana is very skilled in the powers of magic, taught by that little hag dwarf of hers, Miska. Between them they would have been spying on us, you have no idea what they are capable of. They know things and can do things, we can't even imagine and that is why we are all in such danger now. If she knows about us talking to Calem she is certainly going to find out what we have done with her thugs. I am sorry to have to say this but all our lives are now in real danger. She will hunt us down like wild animals until she puts each and every one of us in the earth.'

'Damn that woman,' Calem said, speaking more to himself than anyone else.

'What was it that Hiliron said?'

Inna was thinking out loud.

'We too have powers. Well we're not dead yet and, while there is breath in me, I for one am going to do my utmost to get the Living Stone back'

Inna straightened her back inhaled a deep breath and tensed her jaw; she was ready to take action. She fixed her eyes on Delphine then asked.

'We haven't asked the one important question we all need to know and that is where will we find the stone?'

'I am not a hundred percent sure but there are caves deep down under the palace and I believe that is where she has hidden it.'

'You told Calem his powers of transporting the stone will be useless, why is that?' Inna wanted to know.

'That's right, the one thing I know for sure, with Calem's escape, they will have put a barrier up around the stone that will prevent him from getting anywhere near it.'

Zelda was beginning to fidget, the more she heard the more unsettled she became, it all seemed like an impossible task.

'How do we get to these caves?' Zelda asked a little dismayed. Teka nodded, he also wanted to know.

'Ah, well, there are several ways in. One way is by the sea, there is a cave opening that leads to an underground river you would need to travel along this river until you come to some more caves, somewhere in one of the deepest caves is where the stone will be.

'So what you are saying is, it's like searching for a needle in a haystack,'

Zelda seemed quite upset that Delphine could not be more precise with her information. She was looking over at Inna's pale face and wondered how long she could bear up. She knew the elixirs would not continue to work indefinitely.

'And the other entrance?' Inna asked positively.

'The other entrance to the caves is from the palace through a secret doorway leading down to the caves, very few people know of its existence.'

'But you know,' Calem looked Delphine square in the eyes.

'Yes, yes I do,'

'Will you be willing to help us if we can get ourselves into the palace?'

Calem was working on a plan. Before Define could answer, the horses startled. Everyone turned their attention to the animals.

'Get down.' Calem instructed, he scanned the area behind the horses. He could see a shadow of a figure. Silently he informed Teka and Kadar of what he had seen. How long had they been watched, how many more were out there? Thought Calem. He waved to Teka to go in the opposite direction to himself. They made their way quickly and quietly heading behind the intruder.

Kadar crept towards the horses, all the time the three men kept their eyes on the shadow, it did not move. The nearer Calem got to the shadow the more suspicious he became until finally he could see it was not a man at all but a stuffed sack. It was a trick. Someone had propped a stuffed sack against the tree to look like a man standing, my god it was a trick. Calem quickly turned to where the women were and behind them he could see a figure approaching them, it was a trap. Calem shot up, shouted at the other two, and at the women to warn them of the approaching man, The enemy looked in no mood to take prisoners, he was wielding a sword, and the whooshing sounds could be heard through the air.

All three women backed away from the oncoming slaughter, eyes fixed on their attacker. Panic consumed everyone as it was a certainty that this mad man was going to get one of them, when, to the amazement of everyone, while Zelda and Delphine had turned to run away and while the three men were running towards the brute to fight him off. Inna stood firm and without hesitation she grabbed her crystal from around her neck and raised it in the air to face the sunlight, a pure blinding white light ricochetted off her crystal and shot directly into the oncoming attackers eyes blinding him instantly. He let out a piercing scream and dropped his sword, desperate to shield his eyes from the penetrating rays, but it did no good. He began to claw at his eyes as though he had something in them. All the time Inna stood calmly and still, firmly holding the crystal in her hand. It was not until he flung himself to the ground did she stop.

Calem and Kadar rushed to the helpless attackers side and managed to apprehend him, Inna remained in a daze firmly clasping her crystal, by now all the colour had drained from her face. Teka managed to catch her as she collapsed in a dead faint.

The men tied the attacker to a nearby tree and went over to check on Inna, Zelda had given her some elixir that Abron had given them and she was already starting to feel her strength return.

‘Well,’ Inna said somewhat surprised.

‘I did not know I could do that.’ Calem was thinking it was a good job that she had been able to blind him or the outcome could have been very different, twice now they had been surprised and twice now they had been lucky and escaped any real harm, but things would have to change they were going to have to be more alert, more prepared. It seemed to Calem that each one had skills that, put to the right use, could be useful in helping regain the Living Stone, although he still was not sure what Zelda's were.

‘It's not safe here; there is no telling how many more of Cynthiana's thugs are out there.’

Calem was brushing the dust off himself as he spoke.

‘We must gather as much arms and food and water that we can carry and we must go.’

Delphine looked worried, which did not go unnoticed by the rest of them.

‘It does not matter where we go, she will find us.’

She spoke quietly as if resigning herself to the inevitable fate that would eventually befall her.

‘Yes she might,’ agreed Inna.

‘But I know of a way that will make it more difficult for her.’

‘How?’ They all cried in unison.

'We can put up a wall of blindness around us.'

'Oh and how do you propose to do that?'

There was more than a trace of sarcasm in Calem's voice. It was one thing that she had helped to contain the thug, but now, she was trying to take over. Inna, quickly realising the sensitivity of men, was quick to reassure Calem that without him they would not have survived the past several hours and of course he was in charge but surely they did not have anything to lose by her placing a crystal shield around them to prevent old nosey draws from seeing them. This made Calem laugh and the mood lightened.

'It won't last forever but it should help,' Inna warned.

Calem felt slightly small for questioning Inna and was reminded that she was, after all, The Keeper of the Living Stone and possessed many powers that he did not and although she was very young that did not mean she was not capable of using them, she certainly displayed that with her recent actions. He must remember, furthermore, that this young lady is also Queen of Lithmore and for that reason alone commanded some respect, but apart from that, she had been responsible for saving his people and that made him forever in her debt.

Smiling now, and feeling slightly humbled, Calem instructed the group to get into a circle to prepare to leave. Inna reached into her pouch and pulled out six small pieces of tormilated quartz and placed one piece in each person's left hand leaving one for herself. She then took a stick and drew a circle around them, once it was drawn she stepped into her place within the group and began to chant some words of protection. All the time, everyone stayed still and respectfully confident that Inna knew what she was doing.

Everyone began to feel a tingling sensation in their feet, the earth beneath them gave a little shudder and for a moment each person could feel warmth surging through their bodies, then Inna stepped out of the circle to observe her work. Yes it was done; all she could see was nothing, perfect she thought, stepping back into the circle.

'It's done,' she announced.

'We are ready.'

Calem instructed everyone to hold hands firmly; he did not want to leave anyone behind, a surge of energy rose up and a big flash of light cracked through the air. Within an instant the group had been transported away from Torre Plains.

CHAPTER ELEVEN

'Mistress, mistress, people have already started to arrive at the lake of Prespa.'

Miska was grinning from ear to ear revealing her missing teeth. She jumped onto the chair and reached over to the nearby table and grabbed an apple out of the wooden bowl and began biting down on it.

'I told you they would come,'

Miska was feeling rather pleased with herself. Dwarfs live for many years and this dwarf had waited eons for this time to come, and now it was here, she knew they were close to claiming the mines and she was overjoyed, well, as overjoyed as a dwarf could be.

'That's all very well.' Cynthiana snapped dampening the mood.

'But what has happened to my men that were sent to silence my dear old mother.'

Miska could hear by the tone of her mistress's voice that she was in a foul mood.

'I want to know what is going on Miska. Stop feeding your face and go and find out what has happened to them. Immediately, or I will have cook put you on an open spit for tonight's dinner for the dogs.

Sulkily Miska put her apple down, she knew Cynthiana too well and this was not the time to answer back, she was in a stinky mood and when she was in such a mood anything could happen, usually it ended in a beating. Begrudgingly Miska got off her chair and made her way to the door.

'Very well Malady.'

With her head hung low she made her exit muttering under her breath.

'I can hear you,' screeched Cynthiana.

'Yes Malady.' Miska answered without looking back.

Cynthiana continued to busy herself with her plans; there was much work to be done if they were to take Lithmore and she intended to bring the city to its knees. She would be Queen if it was the last thing she did. Having possession of the gold mines would make her the most powerful person on earth and only then would she feel secure that no one would be a threat to her. The world would be as she wanted and it would be no other way and for those that disobeyed, there would be consequences. How wonderful, she thought, to have possession of the Living Stone, a bonus in her ultimate goal in capturing the mines, perhaps she could force Inna to secure immortality for herself if what they say about the stone is true and it really can bring a person back from the dead. She was not sure how she was going to achieve that but there would be plenty of time to figure that out later, for now there were more important things to do, like seize Lithmore. As she continued to ponder her evil plans she found the Living Stone popping up in her thoughts until finally she decided to return to the cave to take another look at the strange rock.

When she arrived, she found the stone that had shined so bright and seemed so alive when she first saw it, now appeared less vibrant, its illumination was diminishing. This did not please her, for a moment she stood with pursed lips and her eyes squinted fixed in concentration. The Keeper of the Stone was a handed down vocation, she thought. Their job must be to keep it alive. That was it. Not only did the keeper help in the healings, their job must also be to keep the stone alive.

'Well, well.' She spoke the words out loud.

'It seems one is no good without the other.'

'It appears, I need to put "Capture Inna immediately" on my list of things to do, and then they can live happily together as my prisoners.'

She let out a loud wicked laugh that echoed throughout the cave. Contented with her new plans she made her way back to the palace. Excited with how well everything was falling into place. Soon Lithmore would be hers, the gold mines would be uncovered, she would have the Living Stone under her control. All power would be hers, she laughed out loud. Oh yes, she had much to look forward to. Power was exhilarating, and she loved the thrill of a challenge. She would find Inna as soon as possible and bring her to the stone. A cold smirk appeared on her face as she mulled over all her plans.

Miska's room was a little hovel tucked away within the palace grounds, at one time it had been used to keep pigs in but Miska had insisted she live there, she liked it, she was able to have a little garden, which she liked. Inside she had two rooms separated by a doorway covered by a large curtain, one room was used for sleeping, the other her living quarters. As Miska entered her little house she was still muttering to herself, she hated it when her Mistress was displeased with her. She immediately began to fill a large pot full of water and placed it over her fire. On one of the walls of the little hovel there were several selves filled with small bottles, she shuffled over towards them and began pointing her fat little finger up at individual bottles, then she would grunt and move forward and take one of the bottles from the shelf, then she would start the process again, each time pointing her stubby finger at each individual bottle until it seemed one of them made her grunt then she removed it from the shelf. When she had gathered six or seven of these little bottles she took them over to the now boiling water and began to place small contents into the pot. By the fireplace sat a large wooden spoon which she picked up and began to stir the water very slowly, around and around and around, all the time staring into the water.

Gradually a mist began to rise up out of the pot. Miska mumbled satisfactorily to herself as she placed her wooden spoon down and hovered over her work looking intently into her magic. The mist began to fade and once it had all cleared, there in front of her she could see, as real as if she were there, Delphine and Kadar with their hands behind their backs kneeling on the floor about to be beheaded by one of Cynthiana's henchman. Miska rubs her hands with glee, the thought of finally being rid of Delphine pleased her no end, then out of nowhere a group of people appear.

‘It looks like Calem, yes it is Calem, What is he doing there?’ she screams.

The whole scene unfolds in front of her eyes showing her the unbelievable truth of what has become of Cynthiana's men.

‘Who are those people?’ she screams out loud.

‘Who are those people..............?’

She watches in horror as the group defended themselves against trained killers and the unbelievable way a small girl disarms a big lump of a man.

‘My lady is going to be so mad, oh no, This is not good.’ She begins to run around in circles frantically wringing her hands, then clutching her head.

‘I knew we should not have let that stupid old women live. Why couldn't she have eaten the grapes like her stupid, stupid husband, then they would both be dead now. Oh no, what to do, what to do.'

There is a loud bang, Miska looks up to find Cynthiana standing there her hands on her hips and a face like thunder. She had picked up a small pot and banged it on the table to get Miska's attention and now she stood staring, lips tight. Miska froze, her eyes the size of saucers and, for the first time in all the time she had been with Cynthiana, she was frightened of what Cynthiana was going to do. She had never seen such fury in her eyes.

'Move.'

Cynthiana pushed Miska so hard she fell to the ground with a thud. She looked into the pot and learnt everything she needed to know.

'So. That is the new precious Keeper of the Stone.'

Cynthiana could hardly get the words out through gritted teeth.

'Well they are keen to get the Living Stone back. Looks like there is more to Inna than I first thought, but what is this?'

She watches the scene were Inna blinds one of her men then very quickly afterwards collapses. She sees them giving her something to restore her.

'She is weak.'

For a moment Cynthiana is confused, why would a young girl be weak, unless. remembering the stone the way it looked like its life force was leaving it. A young girl collapsing, could it be? Yes, she thought, their life force is connected. One can't live without the other, how extraordinary. I was right they need each other to survive.

'Show me more. I want to know where they are now.'

Miska began to shake as she knew her mistress was going to be displeased when she learnt that Calem and his group, including her mother, had simply vanished.

'How, how is that possible?'Cynthiana screamed as she slammed her fists onto the table.

Miska ran behind her little bed crouching down low in an attempt to hide herself fearing the worst. Containing herself Cynthiana gathered her thoughts.

'Well we can't deal with this now, we have far more important things to do. Come Miska,' and with that she spun around and stormed out of the little hovel.

With a small sigh of relief, Miska obediently emerged from behind the bed and began to follow her Queen who was speedily walking back to her quarters.

'Keep up Miska.'

Miska huffed and puffed behind her, running as fast as her little legs would take her, relieved that she had not been beaten, what was a small pushing, that was nothing, thought Miska and by the time they had arrived back at Cynthiana's chambers her Mistress's mood had changed and she was keen to tell Miska her plans.

'We are going to attack Lithmore in the next few days.'

Miska was confused by this statement as she knew it would take several days for the army to reach the borders of Lithmorian.

'How, how, will our army reach Lithmore in that time?' Miska stammered.

'How is that possible Malady?'

'Our men won't get there stupid. I intend to awake the army of Adreds.'

Miska's eyes sprung open in horror,

'No,...... no Mistress. They are too powerful.'
Miska began to shake. The army of female Adreds cared for no one. Many moons ago Miska had been told the tales of the time before the Adreds were put to sleep how they ravaged the earth, they look harmless enough, until they attack, then their subtle faces turned into monsters, their wings capable of shooting flames, their claws able to extend like sharp razors, their tails like serpent snakes. Just the thought of them filled her dreams with nightmares.

'Malady, surely there must be another way, where we do not have to waken these creatures.'

'Be quiet you sniffling coward, no harm will come to us, I have made sure of that. I will have control over them; they will do exactly what I tell them to do.'

Miska pathetically looked up at Cynthiana who taking pity on her little companion, said,

'Trust me, Miska, all will be well.'

Then she gently patted her on the head. Miska expelled a deep sigh of relief. Her Cynthiana was no longer mad at her and in this moment that was all that mattered. Everything else would sort itself out.

CHAPTER TWELVE

Calem had intended to transport the group just outside Maro's city walls but they found themselves in unfamiliar surroundings amidst a raging storm. As they struggled to get their bearings Delphine shouted above the noise of the wind and the rain.

'This is no place I recognise.'

'Me either, we don't get storms like this in Maro,' exclaimed Kadar.

Confused, Calem scanned his surroundings for any clues as to where they might be, it was certainly hilly, with large groups of trees dotted about. The landscape appeared predominantly green in colour under the dark stormy clouds, not at all like Maro with its flat and arid landscape. He had never made a mistake before, had Inna's wall of blindness interfered in some way? The sky rumbled and began to erupt with loud bursts of thunder and lightning as the wind blew viciously through the tree tops that surrounded them.

The rain pelted down upon their faces; within moments they were all drenched to the skin. That's it, thought Calem, we need to get out of here. He instructed the others to link hands and quickly attempted to transport them from this unknown place to their intended destiny. They stood for what seemed like an eternity, nothing happened, eager faces focused firmly on Calem, his eyes closed with a fierce look of concentration upon his face but still nothing happened. By now they had all began to shake from the cold. Inna was feeling light headed and was experiencing an annoying ringing in her ears but did not want to alarm the others.

'It's no good Calem, it's not working,' cried Zelda,

'We need to find shelter,' her eyes, full of concern, flashed to Inna.

Frustrated, Calem could see Zelda was right. Inna looked awful. They had to find refuge and soon. He had never ever failed to transport and was completely baffled by it but he would have to figure that out later, for now they needed to find somewhere dry to shelter.

Zelda insisted they take the path leading further into the hills and because nobody had a better idea they headed in that direction. The wind and rain continued to pelt down on them, visibility was difficult, Delphine stumbled, Kadar quickly rushed to his Queen's aid and supported her to her feet.

'Thank you.' She mouthed to him.

The ground beneath them felt dangerously slippery, they continued walking arm in arm, Delphine was grateful to have Kadar's strong body to hold onto as they continued to fight against the brutal elements.

The dark clouds were now starting to threaten nightfall, making it increasingly more difficult to find cover from the torrential downpour of rain. The path they were walking became narrower and steeper, eventually they reached the top of the incline only to find the path on the other side of the hill had turned into a small muddy river.

'Well,' said Teka brightly, trying his best to sound positive.

'There seems to be only one way down this hill and that's on our rear ends. We're going to have to slide down this thing. Come on Inna let's be the first,'

Without hesitation he grabbed Inna's hand and held her in front of him, she did not protest as Teka held on tight to her with his arms firmly around her waist.

'Give us a push somebody,' ordered Teka.

Down the hill they went splashing water through the air, so fast, with no way of stopping and, even though Inna was feeling most unwell, the excitement of the journey caused both of them to giggle hysterically until finally they came to a stop on a flat piece of pathway sodden and muddy from the rain.

As the others watched the two youngsters getting up off the ground they could see it was safe to follow. Delphine and Kadar went next followed by Calem and Zelda. Squeals of laughter echoed above the whistling wind as each pair made their way down the hill, water sprayed everywhere soaking their already wet clothes.

With all of them safe at the bottom of the hill they gathered themselves up, the laughter having relieved some tension from this odd predicament they found themselves in, however they still needed to press on, darkness was stealing any remaining daylight and with such menacing clouds in the sky they would have no moon or stars to guide them.

Zelda again insisted on leading the way, this time they all held hands for fear of losing one another, slowly they placed one foot in front of the other, each praying they would find somewhere, anywhere, to get out of this awful storm. By now Inna felt so weak, shaking constantly from the cold, her hands had gone numb, her heart fluttered furiously within her chest and although she was determined to go on she knew she could not take another step and attempted to call to Zelda to tell her so but, before the words could leave her lips, she fell to the ground in a dead faint. Everyone rushed to her side. Teka's heart almost jumped out of his chest. What were they going to do? They had to find the stone and quick but they did not even know where they were. He knelt down beside her gently holding her hand willing her to be ok. This was absolutely crazy here they were lost, they had no idea where they were going. His anger turned to Cynthiana, he briefly thought of what he would do to her if anything happened to his Inna.

'She's unconscious. She's in desperate need of the stone.'

Teka was now consumed with panic.

'We must find shelter and now,' pleaded Zelda.

'What she needs is the stone,' Teka insisted.

'But we can't get her to the stone right now. The best thing we can do is to get her undercover and out of those wet clothes.'

Calem could hear the fear in Zelda's voice, he was well aware that Zelda knew all too well that Teka was right, Inna needed to be connected to the stone, but for now there was nothing she or any of them could do about it.

'I'm frightened we are going to lose her,' whispered Zelda.

'I know.'

Calem reached out and pattered Zelda's shoulder, she grabbed his hand and clung to it for a moment. Calem tried to think. There must be something close by, there just has to be. We have been walking for hours and we still have not found anything, how can that be? If only it wasn't so blessed dark.

Zelda began to get that strange feeling again, an overwhelming feeling of knowing. She pulled on Calem's sleeve.

'We need to go that way.'

She pointed in the direction very close to where they had just come from.

'We have just come from there,' stated Kadar slightly irritated.

He was feeling slightly bemused to why they had all agreed to listen to Zelda in the first place, surely experienced hunters like himself or Calem would have been better qualified to lead the way to find shelter.

'No not quite,' she assured him.

'But that will take us off this path, it will be even more difficult to see where we are going,' argued Teka.

Zelda repeated herself but this time more firmly.

'We must go that way and we must go now.'

Calem looked at Zelda as if she had gone mad.

'Really, we have to go that way?'

Calem sighed as if resigned to Zelda's insistence.

'Ok, that way it is.'

Teka shook his head, why were they listening to Zelda, what did she know about anything, then, suddenly, daylight appeared, a fluttering sound filled the air and to everyone's amazement a swarm of beautiful little creatures hovered above them, everyone looked up, mesmerised.

'They're fireflies,' whispered Delphine.

'Thousands and thousands of them, look they want us to follow them.'

The fireflies began to lead the way lighting a path for them to pursue.

'See.' Zelda sniffed.

'I said we should go that way.'

'Well I'll be.' Calem just shook his head.

'This day is getting weirder by the moment.'

They did not hesitate to follow their new little friends. Calem suggested that they take it in turns carrying Inna.

'I'll go first,' jumped in Teka.

He wasn't about to let Calem or Kadar take care of his Inna. He gently raised her off the ground and as he did so she opened her eyes briefly, and was conscious for a moment, she felt sure she heard children laughing.

They followed the illuminated pathway.

'Something is going on here.' Calem said.

'You think.'

Zelda was being slightly sarcastic but was too captivated by the fireflies to pay him too much attention. She had always loved the little creatures ever since she was a little girl, there was something quite magical about them but to see so many all at once creating a path of tiny lights gave her hope all would be well.

It was not long before they arrived at a large rock with an opening, the fireflies hovered above the doorway as if to say 'This is it, go in.'

'Finally,' exclaimed Teka.

'Shelter at last.'

He did not hesitate and entered into the cave quickly followed by Calem and the others, however Zelda could not enter without first thanking the fireflies for their help, they hovered in front of her creating a huge ball of light then shot up like shooting stars dispersing in a thousand different directions until once more the sky was dark.

Once they were inside the cave they found themselves in a passage, in the distance Calem could see the flicker of a light, he immediately took charge and began to lead the way. As they got closer to the light they could see it was a wall of whirling energy. For a moment they all stopped and stared at it,

‘It's a doorway,’ announced Zelda.

‘We have to go through it,’ she insisted.

‘How do we know if it is safe?’ questioned Teka.

‘We don't, but something has led us here, and whatever it is, I don't think it means to harm us. So, I am willing to risk it and if it means we might be able to help Inna, here goes,’

and without another word Zelda stepped forward and passed through the swirling vortex, leaving stunned faces and mouths wide open in disbelief. Within seconds she reappeared beaming from ear to ear.

‘Wow, come on you lot, you will never believe this.’ She disappeared again.

They all looked slightly confused at each other.

‘Well we should go it's obviously safe,’ remarked Delphine.

Calem shrugged his shoulders as if to agree. Zelda's head appeared through the vortex.

‘Come on, what you waiting for?

Resigned that there was no other option, Calem stepped aside to allow Teka to take Inna through, followed by Kadar and Delphine then finally himself. Before leaving he took one last look back down the dark damp passageway, he could not help but wonder how on earth did they all get here, wherever here was. He was confused, but then, he had been in a state of confusion ever since Cynthiana had used his body to steal the stone.

'Wow.'

'How can this be?'

'This is not possible.'

'I must be dreaming.'

Everyone was talking at once; no one could believe what they were seeing. It was daylight, the sun was shining and the sky was as blue as the sea, a gentle breeze wafted warmly across their faces.

Before them lay a lake with rolling hills in the distance and the gentle sound of waves lapping on the shore seemed to be calling out to them saying, welcome. As they explored, it was as if someone had been expecting them, they found an area with a table and chairs, there were six beds with blankets and dry clothes, food and drinks had been set out, a camp fire was lit with six large logs that had been beautifully carved into seats surrounding it.

'How extraordinary' exclaimed Delphine.' 'Where do you think we are?'

Zelda began to smile to herself, she had an inkling that she knew. Calem, noticing Zelda's face said.

'Well, Miss Zelda, are you going to enlighten us, do you know where we are?'

He misses nothing, she thought looking up into his piercing blue eyes .

'Well, I don't know for sure but, if my instincts are right,'

she paused for a moment, more for dramatic affect than anything.

'I believe we are in the home of the Children of Vision.'

Inna's eyes opened briefly and again she heard the sound of children's laughter, she gave a deep contented sigh and drifted back unconscious. It was true, wherever they were someone had intervened to help them.

They had been provided with food and shelter but when morning had come there was still no sign of anyone. With a general feeling of restlessness they began discussing their concerns for Inna. Zelda and Delphine had managed to make her as comfortable as possible during the night, exchanging her wet clothes for dry and ensuring she was kept warm, she had continued to drift in and out of consciousness but there was no more elixir to revive her and without it fears rose that losing her was becoming a very real possibility, unless they could get her to the stone in time. The mood was bleak. The men were eager to leave and find the stone as soon as possible but unknown to everyone, Calem had already tried to transport without success, wherever they were, for some reason his powers were useless but he was willing to try one more time.

'Maybe, just maybe, we will have a chance of getting her to the stone in time.'

He tried to sound as positive as possible. Having seen Zelda's tired and drained face, it was obvious she was losing hope that they would find the stone in time to save Inna.They all knew that it was a long shot, but it was the only solution they had, so they quickly gathered their things in preparation to leave, when they heard the sound of children giggling. Looking up, they could see no one, and then the giggling got louder. It was Teka who first spotted one of them, hiding behind one of the trees nearby, then Delphine caught a glimpse of two of them running behind the bushes, then they could all see them, they seemed to be everywhere showing themselves as shapes at first then more and more solid until a small group completely revealed themselves as tiny beautiful children of about seven or eight, an illuminating glow radiated from them. A feeling of reverence spread throughout the group as they looked upon these little beings, there appeared to be an inner knowing that they were in the presence of very evolved souls. Even Calem felt quite humbled although he did not quite understand why. A small smiling boy stepped forward.

'Welcome, welcome to our home,'

came the young voice, he looked like any ordinary child with blond hair and blue eyes, yet there was something about him that made him very different to any child they knew.

'Allow me to introduce ourselves. We are the Children of Vision and my name is Ni.'

Calem noticed Zelda's smug look on her face as she had been proven right, they were indeed in the home of the Children of Vision.

'Please be assured that we wish you no harm and that you are safe here,' he continued.

The rest of the children came forward and began to introduce themselves, much chatter broke out and after a short while Ni raised his hand as if to silence everyone, quickly the children hushed and stood very still, it was obvious that Ni had some authority, he then turned his attention to Zelda.

'You have one with you who is gravely ill.'

Zelda nodded, tears began to fill her eyes. The small boy reached out his hand to hers.

'We can help you, that is why we brought you here.'

Zelda nodded her head. She did not know why, but she trusted him, she knew very little about the Children of Vision only what she had learnt as a child through folklore but the problem with folklore is, it is difficult to know what is true and what is not. As a girl she had heard of a race of beings that lived in another dimension, she had heard they take the form of children but that they were extremely evolved and pure beings, they had the gift of seeing all futures, and from time to time they had stepped in and helped mankind in times of great peril, If these truly were the Children of Vision thought Zelda then last night we must have stepped through a porthole bringing us into their world.

'That's correct,' answered Ni.

Zelda stared at the young boy, he had read her thoughts. Ni grinned.

'We know of a way we can help Inna.'

Of course he knows her name, thought Zelda and for the first time since the disappearance of the stone Zelda felt real hope that these small children could really help their beloved Inna. Ni turned to addressed the whole group.

'We know what has to be done. We know of a way to take your friend to the stone where her energy can merge with that of the stone so that they will both be healed and renewed. We can also teach her how to do this in case she needs to do this again in the future.'

The look of utter disbelief showed upon all of their faces.

'I thought you said you were unable to leave this place.'

Teka spoke more out of frustration, as the pain in his heart was getting bigger by the moment as he watched the life force ebb away from Inna. He was desperate to believe Ni but unable to understand what he was saying was possible. Ni simply smiled at him and the children giggled which only succeeded in making Teka cross.

'Let me explain. It is true we can't physically leave this dimension but we have mastered the art of Astral Travel, where we can travel anywhere in time and space not in our physical bodies but in our etherial bodies, it's very liberating. Now in Inna's case we must take her as she is too weak to do it for herself but in the future she too will know how to release her ethereal body to travel where she needs to go. I can't tell you if the healing she will receive will be as powerful as if she was there in the physical but I feel sure it will work well enough.'

Zelda's eyes were full of hope, she believed that these small Children were indeed going to be able to bring dear Inna back to them well and strong. Teka was not so convinced.

'There is one thing you should all know.'

Ni's tone became very serious, she will be safe with us, but in the future when she needs to return to the stone, you will be the ones who will have to protect her. You must understand this, it is essential that you protect her physical body while she is gone.'

They all nodded their heads feeling more like the children than the child speaking to them.

'Now we must act quickly, as you can see time is running out, we must take her now.'

Several of the children went to where Inna was laying and gently picked her up and carried her off out of view. Calem took a deep intake of breath, slightly unsure about the whole situation, he looked towards Zelda who seemed calm and confident in what these small children were doing. Ni confronted Calem.

'Trust us,' was all he said.

There was no Inna to assure him that what Ni was saying was the truth, but they had led them to safety and provided them with food and shelter. Time had run out for Inna, there were no more choices; Calem knew he must trust these children. With a swift nod of his head he gave his permission. Ni smiled, and then turned to leave. The five of them stood watching as the last child faded out of sight, silent, each with their own thoughts. Without thinking Calem placed his arm around Zelda's shoulder, gently pulling her towards him, she did not resist but gently rested her head on his shoulder. No words were spoken.

Once the Children were in a safe secluded area, they gently laid Inna's unconscious body onto the soft dry grass. Ni and Klio, a tiny red headed little girl with rosy cheeks took up positions lying one each side of Inna. They both held one of Inna's hands then closed their eyes. The rest of the children formed a circle around them. For a moment everything was very still, then a thin white copy of their bodies rose up out of their physical bodies and fluttered like butterflies for a moment then they vanished.

Ni and Klio could see immediately they arrived in the cave that the Living Stone was near death, its lifeforce almost diminished, they looked at each other fearing they may be too late to save either Inna or the stone. Quickly they laid Inna's ethereal body onto the stone then stood back and waited. Nothing happened, they waited a little while longer and still nothing happened.

They stayed hoping against hope but after many hours their own strength began to decrease and the need for them to return to their own bodies became a matter of survival. This was dreadful; they had been too late to save Inna and the stone. Ni and Klio shook their heads, they were going to have to return and break the news. This was terrible, terrible. Ni had been so confident, he was never wrong, yet here was his proof Inna lay lifeless and the stone was almost black in colour.

Just as they were about to leave they noticed a small glimmer of light shimmer from the stone. They stared in disbelief, the light grew bigger and within seconds it burst into light setting the whole cave aglow. Inna rose up from the stone and began to swim in the air above it, beautiful radiant colours began swirling around her, pinks, blues, yellows, lavender, Ni sighed a huge sigh of relief. Klio smiled from ear to ear, then to their surprise the cave filled with the sound of singing; they had never heard anything like it, it was the most captivating music they had ever heard and it was coming from Inna. The children began to jump for joy.

After a while the wonderful sound of Inna's voice began to fade into silence and the swirling colours ceased, Inna descended with her feet on the ground, the Living Stone pulsated a beautiful radiant light, they watched as Inna stood before the Living Stone she was smiling, renewed.

'Umm umm,' Ni gently tried to get Inna's attention.

'We have to return now.'

Inna looked at him slightly confused; she was not sure what was going on. This was all feeling very real. Was it a dream, no it is too real for that, she thought? Somehow I am here in this cave with my beloved stone, yes I am here she repeated to herself, she looked into Ni's eyes, the eyes of a child, she remembered hearing children's laughter. These children have helped me, she thought. Instantly she felt trust towards them as Ni and Klio held out their hands towards her, she felt no hesitation in placing her hand in theirs. Immediately she felt a sharp pull and for a moment felt dizzy and a little off balance, then she could feel a warm breeze on her face. Opening her eyes she found herself surrounded by a large circle of smiling children.

There was no mistaking the sounds of the approaching children as their laughter echoed through the air. Zelda and the others were delighted to see Inna walking tall amongst them led by a smiling Ni. These special children had succeeded in bringing their Inna back to them.

CHAPTER THIRTEEN

Inna returned to the group a changed girl. The children had succeeded in taking Inna's ethereal body and connecting her to the Living Stone, it had worked, both she and the stone had been rejuvenated and now it was as if the sun shone through her, she was well and so full of life again. Zelda felt completely satisfied that the Children of Vision had successfully found a way to keep Inna safe until she and the stone could truly be reunited and safely returned to Lithmore but her curiosity was aroused and she was eager to learn more about these extraordinary beings and their unearthly ways. The opportunity to learn more came while she and Klio were relaxing beside the lake, splashing their feet into the water; Klio was using her arms for props to hold herself in an upright position with her head hung back. Zelda just lay on the ground extending her feet into the water enjoying the earth beneath her and the sensation of the water flowing through her toes. Together they basked in the sun enjoying each other's company.

Klio explained that they were a race of very old evolved souls that lived on a separate plain to that of Zelda and the others, that in fact many separate plains existed, all with gateways leading in and out of them, however these gateways were not easy to find. It had not been accidental that Zelda and the group had found the gateway that led them to the Children of Vision's home. The children had in fact been responsible for them finding it. Klio spoke of Zelda's intuitive powers and because of her intuitiveness she was able to pick up on the vibration of them calling to her.

'It did not matter that you knew why you should travel a certain way, it was enough that you trusted your inner voice to lead the others. Your feelings of being impelled to follow a certain path that night was you listening to us calling to you,' explained Klio.

'Your Senses were so strong you insisted your way was the right way to go.'

'That is so true. Teka did not want to listen to me but I wasn't having any of it. I just knew we were going to find shelter, I felt something was pulling me in the direction we followed.' Zelda smiled at her little friend.

'That was us calling to you. Help does not always come to us in words or visions, sometimes we have to still ourselves and use our other senses such as how we feel. So often people miss warnings and inspirations because they don't trust or listen to what their inner self is saying and sometimes screaming at them.' They both laughed.'

'So what about the fire flies?'

'Oh we could see Teka and the others were beginning to doubt you and you were so close to the cave opening we sent you a little help.' They both laughed again.'

Zelda was glad she had listened to her inner voice that night and that they had found the Children of Vision and that her dear Inna was once more safe and well, but she still found her mind was full of unanswered questions, sitting up, she began to splash her feet nervously in the water before carrying on.

'Tell me Klio, why did you really bring us here?'

Klio seemed slightly uncomfortable by this question and began to fidget nervously, she turned to face her new friend and studied her for a moment before answering.

'We have been watching you for some time.'

‘Do you mean you interfered with Calem's transporting.’

Klio looked a little guilty,

‘I am afraid we did, but I must quickly say it was for a good reason, I am not at liberty to tell you, Ni wants to speak with you all. What I can say is that your world is in much danger, and the world of others may eventually be in trouble if she is not stopped.’

Klio quickly put her hand over her mouth realising she had said too much.

‘Please go on.’

Klio shook her head. ‘I mustn't.’

‘Please.’ Zelda pleaded.

Giving in, Klio continued.

‘As you know, we appear as children and we have many childlike ways but we are very old souls, we maintain child bodies to keep our energies pure and innocent, this way it allows us to have very keen powers of perception. We receive illuminated visions of the future. All futures may be altered depending on the choices of the individuals concerned; however once in a while a single person comes along who has the power to change thousands of people’s lives by their actions. Something must be done to stop her or she will corrupt the future with her wickedness and unleash such evil upon your world that it will eventually seep into ours and other worlds destroying everything, including herself eventually.’

For a moment Zelda sat in stunned silence, horrified as Klio could only be referring to one person. Cynthiana, could she really be that powerful, wondered Zelda. Her heart beat faster as the harsh realisation sank in that their objective was not just about reuniting Inna with the Living Stone and returning it to Lithmore. This was a much bigger task for them all to tackle before they could reach the end of their journey.

The pleasant feeling of earlier raced away to be replaced by a haunting feeling of uneasiness. She must find out more, but before she could try Teka interrupted them putting a swift end to their conversation.

'Ni has asked me to come and fetch you both; apparently he has something he has to say to us all.'

Obediently both females raised up off the ground and followed Teka to where Ni and the others were.

'Ah, good, I see we are all here, I would ask you all to follow me.'

Zelda glanced at Calem questioningly, he just shrugged his shoulders, he had no idea what was going on. Nevertheless they all followed the small child unquestioningly

Ni and the children were carrying lit torches and the reason for this became clear as they entered a dark cave; they could see their shadows dancing on the walls. Ni led the group followed by the rest of the children at the rear. They made their way deeper and deeper into the cave. It felt damp and cold and they could hear the sound of running water falling from the walls. Shallow pools of water covered the ground and everybody got wet feet. Calem began to wonder what on earth Ni was up to.

'Where are you taking us?' he asked.

'All's well.'

Was all Ni replied as he continued walking at a brisk pace with very poor light to guide them. Calem tutted to himself not convinced, Zelda however was by now beginning to trust her inner feelings and felt they were in no danger, she reached out to Calem and squeezed his arm to reassure him, he grabbed her hand and squeezed it back, he knew no matter how sinister this place was, if Zelda and Inna trusted young Ni then he trusted their judgment. He had learnt that much about these two women, their instincts were spot on.

Suddenly Ni stopped he had brought them all to a dead end. In front of them a huge black rock blocked their passage, it looked like shiny hematite and as they stared at it they could see their reflections peering back at them. Now Calem was really confused and something seemed to be exciting the children, as they began to chat their voices got louder and louder until Ni raised his hand and silence was restored.

He turned towards the shiny rock then stepped forward and began to speak in a language that none of them understood then stretched his hand out and began tracing imaginary symbols in the air. Everyone watched intently, eager to see what was going to happen. A rumbling sound began; surprised gasps were heard as a large crack emerged down the centre of the rock and began to separate revealing another doorway filled with swirling energy. The visitors were surprisingly unafraid as Ni turned to them with his endearing smile, and then waved his hand to indicate that they follow him through the doorway. Without question or fear each one followed him.

They found themselves in a corridor with a white marble floor and dimly lit, again the group could hear the excited tones of the children as they reached a large wooden door. Ni was the first to enter. The women gasped and the men just stared as they stepped through the doorway taking in the beauty of their surroundings. They were no longer in a cave because daylight was all around them. They were standing on a white marbled floor, each side of them stood tall clay arches that led out onto gardens, they could see a host of flowers, bold in colour unfamiliar to anything they had seen before. The flowers seemed to radiate an energy that they could all feel and it was very pleasant. They could also see fountains, and beautifully formed trees, the sound of birds singing filled the air as they made their way along the corridors, looking out at the beautiful flowers and trees, Inna could not help being reminded of her own enchanting gardens at Lithmore and, for a moment, she felt homesick longing to be back there. She missed

Hiliron and Abron, she missed watching the people in the market place going about their daily lives, she missed the priests that rarely spoke but always smiled at her but most of all she missed her Grandmother, she gave a big sigh.

Ni led them into a large circular room. Looking up everyone could see the most dazzling glass dome with every colour of the rainbow, many doorways led from this room. It was clear this was a meeting place of some sort, benches were lined up row upon row, and in the centre of the room appeared to be a stage. The children grabbed the hands of their visitors and lead them to the front row where they all sat obediently. Ni disappeared for a moment then returned with a large book in his hand. He made his way to the front of the stage where he placed the book on a pedestal in front of him.

A hush filled the room. Calem, although very grateful for everything the children had done for Inna, was eager to get on and find the stone. He began to fidget restlessly in his seat. Zelda, sensing his unease, placed her hand on his knee. He immediately knew she was asking for his indulgence in allowing the children their moment to talk to them. With all the excitement with Inna she had not had time to relay what Klio had told her. There was a little cough from Ni,

‘Our dear welcomed guests,’ he began.

‘You see children here before you and that may lead you to think that we are not capable of wisdom.’

He paused for a moment and puffed his chest out like an old man. Calem could not resist smiling, but quickly paid attention when Ni looked at him.

‘It was not an accident that you came to us.’

Delphine and Kadar looked surprised; Teka and Inna squeezed each other's hands, as if things were starting to make sense to them, and Calem just rolled his eyes.

‘You and your people are in mortal danger.’

Ni finally had Calem's attention.

‘The Living Stone is a precious wonderful gift that has been given to you all, and it is natural to think that your only mission is to rescue it, and return it to its rightful place at Lithmore, and so it is, one of your tasks, but, my dear ones, you have a much bigger undertaking before your mission is complete, and that is the task of defeating the one who stole the stone.’

For a moment Delphine thought her heart had stopped. Kadar grabbed hold of her hand and held in tight.

‘She has set a course so evil, so destructive, that it will not only affect your world but the world of others.’

‘She will never succeed,’ Calem jumped in.

‘We have an army marching in on Maro to help recover the stone, her men will never get past them, so they will never be able to take Lithmore. We know what she wants and she won't succeed.’

‘I am afraid you are wrong Calem, she has every intention of succeeding and no army of men will stop her.’

Everyone began to protest that it was not possible, Lithmore’s army was the most powerful of all armies she would never defeat it. Ni could feel the tension and anger rising but he knew that his new friends must learn all the facts if any of them were to stand a chance in the future, all their lives depended on the outcome of this one woman's actions. His young face, for the first time, took on the appearance of a very wise and knowing personality, his eyes fixed on their faces, and he felt sad as he knew they had a mammoth task ahead of them. He continued.

‘Please listen. She has determined to wake the army of Adreds.’

There was a sharp intake of breath from everyone, as they had all heard the stories of when they had last been awake and roamed the earth, evil horrible creatures that would rip a human apart in seconds then eat them. Frightened murmurs' were heard.

'How could she do such a thing?'

Ni heard one of them say.

Delphine sat with her head hung low, ashamed that it was she who was responsible for bringing this despicable creature into the world. Kadar desperately wanted to take her pain away from her, knowing she did not deserve to feel such grief. Ni, realising the situation, pressed on conscious of Delphine being present.

'We as the Children of Vision, see the future, but as you may know there are many possible futures, for now we have to concentrate on the possible outcome of this one for the sake of all mankind. It is too late to prevent the Adreds from being awoken. That deed is done. Our objective now must be to ensure that they are placed back into their sleep state forever.'

It was too much, Calem stood up and began to protest. How were they, just a handful of people, going to be able to stop the Adreds, they did not stand a hope. They had no weapons powerful enough to destroy them; thousands of lives would be lost.

'We know you may be forced into battle with these creatures and sadly we believe there will be loss of life but there is hope. There is a way of getting rid of these Adreds.'

Ni immediately had everyone's attention.

'There is a word, if spoken by a pure heart, will banish the Adreds forever.'

Almost in unison everyone asked.

'What is the word?'

'We don't know what it is but we do know who does, and where you must go to find it.'

Calem recoiled into his thoughts, frustrated at the absurdity of the situation how was it possible that a pure heart voicing one word was going to be able to overpower such a force as the Adreds. He could not help thinking the whole situation would be laughable if it wasn't so serious he was full of doubt that such a thing was possible. He understood fighting, combat, but whispering unknown words, how was that possible? He remembered the stories from his childhood of the Adreds, they were the cause of his nightmares. He tried to recall how they had been put to sleep in the first place, then remembered it had been just one man who had managed it. Perhaps it was possible for one person to put a stop to them. Just then he remembered the name of the man, Dar the only living person who had been able to rid the earth of these terrifying creatures, Dar, as he recalled the story, was a nomad that roamed the earth with no apparent home he had been a master of many things to do with mysticism and magic. Calem's attention returned to Ni as he heard him mention Dar's name.

'We believe this man passed this knowledge onto the Key Nymph for safe keeping and she is who you must find.'

Ni went on to explain that they would need to go in search of the Nymphs and they could be found on the Lithmorian plains in the south region amongst the groves. Zelda became very excited as she knew the area, her father had taken her there as a child to swim in the warm springs that could be found there. A small ray of hope rose up within everyone, although they all had very mixed emotions. Inna was anxious to be reunited to the stone and return back to her beloved Lithmore, she desperately wanted things back to the way they were although she knew that was never going to happen, things would never be the same for her again. She had big responsibilities and she was being forced to face up to them. Teka's main concern was to keep Inna safe he felt unprepared for what surely lay ahead of them all. Delphine's shame overwhelmed her, she felt responsible for the whole situation they found themselves in and Zelda felt consumed with apprehension. It did not matter what the other was feeling, they all knew one thing for certain and that was action had to be taken.

Before they could go in search of the Nymphs they decided they must get word to Hiliron to warn him that Cynthiana had woken the Adreds. Calem calculated that the army would not be able to return to Lithmore in time to stop the Adreds. Lithmore would only have its townspeople and a few soldiers to protect it from these monsters somehow they would have to come up with a plan to delay the Adreds' onslaught of the city. Ni agreed it would be wise to warn Hiliron first. At least that way they may stand a chance if they could manage to put up a barrier of some type, it could buy them some time. That settled the decision was made they would all return back to Lithmore immediately.

Leaving the Children of Visions home was not going to be as straightforward as Calem had hoped, as he discovered, that he could not transport on this plain, and that they would have to leave and re enter into their own world for him to be able to accomplish this. Time was of the essence so everyone gathered their things as quickly as possible and the children led them to the gateway. Everyone quickly said their goodbyes.

‘How can I ever thank you for all you have done for us, especially me.’ Inna was talking to Ni and Klio.

Both children laughed and assured her no thanks was needed.

‘If we all survive this, and if, in the future there is anything you need call out to me and I will come.’

‘So will we’ chorused the others.

Again the children laughed.

‘And how do you propose we do that?’ asked Ni.

Inna took the small boys hand and placed it on her crystal that hung around her neck.

‘If this crystal ever turns red, then I shall know you need us. How does that sound.’ Both Ni and Klio beamed.

‘That sounds good,’ they echoed in unison.
Zelda touched Inna's arm then gently stroked Klio's face.

‘We must go.’

One by one they each returned to their own world smiling and waving at the children as they went.

CHAPTER FOURTEEN

Returning to their own world they found themselves in the exact storm they had left behind, it was as if time had stood still. The wind was gushing and the rain pelted down on their faces, within seconds they were all soaked to the skin. Calem still did not have a clue where they were but he felt confident that now he could finally transport everyone. He was acutely aware they needed to get back to Lithmore as soon as possible to warn Hiliron of the Adreds. The dark sky made it almost impossible to see and the sound of the wind blowing made such a noise it was difficult to hear.

Calem shouted as loud as he could for everybody to hold on to each other. Obeying his instructions everyone huddled in close. When he was assured that everyone was connected Calem successfully removed them from the unknown place that had led them to the enchanting Children of Vision.

Hiliron awoke to the sound of a commotion in his chambers. He sleepily opened his eyes rubbing them in disbelief at the sight before him. Six bedraggled looking figures stood in the middle of his chamber. He quickly sat himself up in bed.

'You're all wet.' Hiliron said, stating the obvious.

He Jumped out of bed and rushed over to the figures standing in pools of water. Thank goodness he had remembered to put his nightgown on, he thought. Inna threw her arms around him.

'Have you found the stone, are you well?'

He was searching Inna's face, she looked well, that was a good sign, he thought.

'No we have not found the stone yet,' Inna replied,

Hiliron's heart sank,

'But I am ok, I have been with the stone.'

Hiliron was now confused.

'We have so much to tell you Hiliron, but if you don't mind, I think we should get into some dry clothes first.'

'Oh, yes of course. '

Inna hugged Hiliron again and assured him she was truly ok and that they would explain everything when they returned.

'Meet me in the hall in twenty minutes.' Hiliron shouted after them.

Poor Hiliron was left alone in his room staring down at a pool of water left by his visitors and eager to find out all the news, he was also curious to learn more of the two strangers that had returned with the others. It struck him they would all be hungry; he decided he would arrange for food to be taken to the hall, he quickly got dressed and hurried off about his task.

In their eagerness to return to Hiliron everyone had gathered back at the hall quickly and were surprised to be greeted with tables full of lovely inviting food which they eagerly tucked into as they were all famished. Calem was enjoying a beer when Abron appeared. There was much to tell these two wise men but firstly they had to formerly introduce Delphine and Kadar to them.

At first Hiliron felt a little wary of Delphine until he heard the whole story, of how Cynthiana had treated her, that she too was a victim in all this. He shook his head in horror at the thought, that one's own child could order the execution of their own parent, how sad, shocking, he thought.

He had heard tales of the Children of Vision but did not know that they really existed and was fascinated to hear everything about them; he felt quite envious and wished he could meet them to thank them for saving Inna but the serious news everyone was eager to communicate to Hiliron and Abron stole both the men's attention. The outrageous discovery of Cynthiana's plans, Neither one of them had any knowledge of gold in the Lithmorian region, there had never been any whispers or tales or any hint whatsoever that there was gold anywhere in the area. The secret of it must have been buried for a very long time, thought Hiliron. But of course they had not heard the most disturbing news of all yet, and that was that Cynthiana had awoken the Adreds. Hiliron and Abron became visibly ashen.

'How much time do you think we have before they get here?'

Hiliron directed his question to Calem.

'Well the good thing is they only fly at night. I would say we have less than twenty four hours.'

'Oh dear, that does not leave us very long. And you say the only way we can stop them is by using a word and a specific word at that, and that this word has to be obtained. That seems remarkable considering the power these creatures have, that one word could be so powerful to silence them.'

Hiliron placed his head in his hands to try and concentrate his thoughts.

'And you say only a pure heart can receive the word?' he asked.

Calem nodded his head the others agreed. Hiliron was well aware that Inna would be the best chance of gaining the word as she had the purest heart, that would mean she would have to leave again as he was pretty certain the Nymph would not pass the word onto anyone else except a pure heart. The only blessing, he thought, was she did appear much stronger but how long would that last, the stone and she still needed their life force connected and how soon that would be no one knew. From what he had been told, when the time comes, Inna will need to be protected while she leaves her body to go to the Living Stone and if that is the case she will need all the help she can get. That would mean all six of them leaving to go in search of the Key Nymph.

His most immediate problem now, as he could see it, was how were they going to protect Lithmore from the Adreds. After much discussion it was agreed they should send out word to the outside villages immediately to gather the people into the city for protection. They would arm themselves and lay down fire traps, once everyone was safe within the walls. Women and children would be hidden deep within the palace for as much protection as possible and the men would remain to protect the city. But these weren't soldiers, they were merchants, and old men, and boys. Then Inna came up with a brainwave.

'We can build a wall off blindness like we have against Cynthiana finding us.'

Everyone, who by now was on the verge of exhaustion, sprang to attention. Inna was right, so far, the wall of protection had seemed to work. Was it possible to do the same to a city? Could Inna manage to hide a whole city from the eyes of the world, especially from the eyes of the Adreds. It was worth a try and, even though there was no knowing how long it would last, surely it would buy them some time.

The decision was made. Inna would attempt to put up a wall of blindness around the city. There was no time to sleep even though it was the early hours of the morning, messengers rode out on horses to all the nearby villages, waking sleepy confused people out of their beds, expressing the urgency of leaving their homes and making their way to the city of Lithmore immediately.

All the priests were called to the temple. Inna knew if she was going to succeed with her wall of blindness she was going to need their help, she knew they had a good understanding of crystal energy and that they were also masters at chanting, skilled in using vibrational harmonics to increase energy. She believed between the sound and the crystal energy they could manage to build a wall of blindness powerful enough to hide Lithmore. if only for a short while, enough to buy them some time.

Unsure why they had been asked to gather over the sacred burial site of the Keepers of the Stone the priests stood about in small groups speaking to one another in hushed tones. A feeling of apprehension filled the air; they knew people had been sent out to the villages to gather everyone within the city walls and one or two of them had heard whispers of an approaching attack.

Their heads all turned as Inna entered the temple, her back straight, her head held high, she looked far more confident than she felt. Teka watched from a distance as Inna walked amongst the priests into the centre of the circle. They all began to mumble to each other, Inna's tall slim figure could be seen by most of the priests as she raised her hand in the air. All fell quiet. She explained to them the importance of building a shield around Lithmore and the reason for doing so and although none of the priests had ever known of an Adred to exist in their life, they had heard stories that shot fear into their hearts. They all quickly understood the importance of successfully creating a wall of blindness around Lithmore for protection from these evil creatures.

'We know what it is that we have to do, to permanently rid the earth of these horrid monsters but, in the meantime, it is vital that we protect Lithmore. I believe with your help we can do this, my intention is that we shall create a wall of blindness around the city so that these creatures cannot find us. I believe this could give us some much needed time to achieve what we must do to put an eternal end to this nightmare.'

An elderly priest stepped forward.

'Tell us what you want us to do Inna, and it will be done.'

The entire group of priests nodded their heads. Inna searched the faces of these men, their whole lives dedicated to healing, prayer, and meditation, their only thirst was for knowledge and their only ambition to pass that knowledge on. These were good kind men; she gave a gentle smile of appreciation.

‘Thank you. I don't know if it is going to work, but with your help we stand a chance.’

She took a deep breath, then pursing her lips she braced herself to proceed. Firstly she took aside the elder priests and spoke with them separately. Teka could see them every now and again nod their heads. They then gathered the others to them and, speaking in low tones, they appeared to be giving instructions to one another. Inna called Teka to her, he was holding two bags in his hands, the priests cleared a path so he could take them to her. She opened the bags and began to pull out handfuls of crystals which she passed out to all the priests. Once they had all been given a piece of tourmalated quartz and a small piece of garnet to hold in their hands they all moved to the edge of the circle and began to walk slowly clockwise. Inna remained in the centre of the circle.

The priests began to chant the Om sound, the rhythm of the music calming and reassuring at first, each priest holding their precious stones in their open hands cupped in front of them as if making an offering. Teka, who had the privilege of witnessing this powerful ceremony, thought it was the most beautiful thing he had ever seen or heard. The volume of the Om sound getting increasingly louder, the priests began melting into a sea of colour as their bright robes blended into one another creating a swirl of colour. Inna stood holding in front of her a large crystal point, Teka could already see a white light radiating from it. The sound of the Om now resonating throughout the whole of the temple. The priests stop walking and turn inwards to face Inna. The light is so bright and the sound is so powerful Teka can no longer see the shapes of priests or Inna they have all merged into swirling light. The energy has become so powerful and overwhelming that Teka finds himself spinning and then nothing. He falls to the floor in a dead faint.

Poor Teka is not trained or knowledgeable enough to cope with such energies, it all becomes too much for him. Meanwhile the temple continues to fill with a brilliant white light, the resonating Om sound can be heard but no priest or Inna can be seen, all have become pure energy.

Out in the street of Lithmore people could sense the emerging surge of energy, men, women and children stand still, fixed in a trance like state, unable to move, the ground beneath begins to shake toppling over pots and various small items. Hiliron and Calem look at each other. She is doing it, she is managing to put up a shield they could feel it. A whoosh of white light ricocheted throughout the whole city.

Teka rubs his head as he peers at the circle, the priests and Inna are standing quite still. They all look so peaceful. Inna opens her eyes and begins to smile; the priests are all smiling to and begin patting each other on the back congratulating each other on their success. Inna stands giving thanks silently to herself, but knowing she must get back to the others.

Teka can see Inna scanning the temple, she is looking for him, he waves his hand at her, as soon as she sees him she turns to thank the priests and makes her way as quickly as possible towards him.

'Are you ok?' Teka asked, concerned as always.

'Yes, yes, I am fine, we must get back to the others.'

Teka put out his hand to take Inna's.

'You look pale, do you need to connect with the stone?'

'No, no, there is no time, I'm ok. We have to find the Nymphs. Please Teka, stop worrying.'

Inna's pallor did not go unnoticed by the others on her return to the great hall but Inna was determined nothing was going to disrupt their plans. If they were going to stand a chance against the

Adreds they must leave immediately in search of the Key Nymph, there was no telling how long it was going to take to find her and there was no telling how long the wall of blindness was going to last.

CHAPTER FIFTEEN

Calem successfully transported everyone to the area that the Children of Vision had described to them. It was certainly a place of beauty, the temperature here however appeared cooler and the air fresher. Tall majestic trees stood amongst wide open spaces and in the distance snow capped mountains dominated the landscape. For a moment everyone seemed lost in their breathtaking surroundings.

'Where do we go from here?' asked Teka eagerly.

Having drawn everyone's attention to the reason for being there, much discussion broke out as to which direction should be taken until Zelda, who had remained quiet, firmly and assuredly announced they would all be heading north. They all shut up and stared at her, no one questioned her, all debate was dropped and they began to make their way north. None of them knew how far they were going to have to go or how long it was going to take but surprisingly the mood was cheerful as they went in search for the Key Nymph. The sun beamed down upon them and it was impossible not to enjoy the pleasurable surroundings they found themselves in.

As they walked along, they breathed in the fragrances of all the wild flowers and delighted in the many different butterflies that seemed to be in this area, it was easy to forget the reason that had brought them to this place and difficult to imagine, in an environment so serene, such dark forces as the dreaded Adreds could even exist. It was an easy walk and the mood amongst everyone remained bright and cheerful considering the great threat that loomed over them. Even though Delphine and Kadar were the oldest they were good strong walkers and in no way slowed the others down, but the younger ones were beginning to get tired and a little anxious that they had not found any sign of a Nymph yet. It seemed they had been walking for hours when the perfect opportunity came for a rest as they came across a small stream, they decided to stop to fill up their water bottles and eat some of the food they had brought with them.

Inna sat quietly immersed in her thoughts. Zelda's motherly instincts began to kick in, she could see how pale and drawn Inna had become, she feared Inna must not leave it much longer before connecting to the stone, or she would be too weak to astral travel. She was just about to suggest to Inna that they make a safe place for her when Inna interrupted her thoughts.

'I need to go,' her face seemed full of apprehension.

Zelda, patted her hand, pleased she had made the decision herself.

'Well you know what to do. You will be fine,' Zelda smiled reassuringly.

They all knew it would not take long but the sooner it was done the better. A comfortable place on the ground was made and a thin blanket was wrapped around her to keep her feeling warm and secure. Everyone sat around her in a circle with their backs towards her keeping guard. No one spoke, the only noise that could be heard was the rustle of the leaves in the trees and the birds singing and the gentle sound of the water from the nearby stream that created a soothing and relaxing environment. It did not take long for Inna to drift off into a deep sleep where she could then take her astral self off to reunite with the Living Stone.

Slight concerns began to creep in with each passing hour. They were sure Inna should have returned by now and, even though her body looked peaceful enough as she lay on the ground, there was no indication of movement, her breathing appeared so shallow, Zelda had to lean forward to check that she was really breathing. They all stared at her lifeless body, willing her back safe with them.

They began talking amongst themselves in low tones and Teka began pacing nervously, always keeping a watchful eye on Inna, fearing some form of intruder might frighten her. The Children of Vision had made it quite clear that she must not be shocked awake as the trauma could harm her severely. Calem could not stop himself from trying to calculate how close they might be to finding the Nymphs, when all of a sudden the ground began to shake, the earth began to rip apart and bushes began to grow all around them.

Everyone rushed to Inna's side to protect her. The trees and bushes sprung up completely surrounding them, Calem felt like a deer in a trap. Panic surged through Zelda's veins, she knew she must not wake Inna she must come back to them in her own way but would this shaking ground jolt her back and if so what harm could come to her, How on earth do you protect her from this, she thought.

The bushes got taller and stole the light from them. Eventually the rumbling stopped, the trees and bushes fully grown, they found themselves completely surrounded and caved in.

‘Do you think she is ok?’ Teka was almost frantic with worry.

‘She seems ok,’ soothed Delphine who patted Teka on the shoulder.

‘It's hard to tell though, it’s so dark in here,’ Kadar piped in.

‘Well let’s bring some fire near her and we can get a better look.’

Delphine made it her business to make fire and bring it closer to Inna to try and assure Teka and the others that Inna was still ok, but, before she had a chance to complete her task, she could hear the gentle tones of Inna's voice.

‘I must have been gone hours if it is the middle of the night.’

Nervous laughter broke out.

'Oh Inna, thank goodness you are back with us.'

Delphine embraced the confused young girl.

'What's going on and where are the stars?'

Again they all laughed this time louder. Teka was eager to explain it was not night she was seeing.

'This odd thing just happened. We are completely surrounded by all these trees and bushes they are so tall they have stolen all the daylight from us.'

Delphine flashed her torch so that everyone could see, Inna gazed around and sure enough they were completely surrounded, there was no sign of the little stream, nothing, but trees and bushes.

'What the' Calem had spotted something he sprung to his feet and dashed over to investigate followed by Teka. It looked like a small opening, yes, it was an opening.

'There's a path out of here. Come on you lot, let's go.'

Quickly everyone gathered their belongings and followed one by one after Calem who had taken the lit torch from Delphine to light the way. They followed a corridor of bushes and trees that stood several feet tall, first they seemed to walk one way then they seemed to come back on themselves.

'I think we are going around in circles here.' Delphine suggested.

'No, I think we are in a labyrinth of some kind.' Zelda announced.

'We must be close to the Nymphs,' exclaimed Inna.

'You are,' spoke a female voice.

'You are, you are.' said another voice.

‘What did you say Delphine?’

‘I didn't say anything.’

‘Odd I could have sworn you just said something.’

Teka felt a hand stroke his face, his head shot around he knew no one had touched him so what was that. Then he felt someone blow in his ear sending shivers up his spine.

‘Wow, what's going on here?’ Everyone looked at him.

‘What's wrong?’ asked Inna.

‘Did you see or hear anything?’ They all shook their heads.

‘Ok, then it must be my imagination, this is very spooky.’

The group hurriedly continued their journey trying to find their way out of the enclosed pathway, everyone was feeling uneasy and eager to escape out of this entrapment. In Calem's haste he felt a hand pat his bottom he swung his head around and glared at Zelda whose eyes were focused forward in fierce concentration. Odd, thought Calem, he had felt sure he had felt a hand on him but it was an odd time to be playing games, and by the look on Zelda's face, it certainly had not been her who had done it.

‘Teka, did you say you heard a voice.’ They all stopped to listen.

‘Yes, yes and I felt something blow in my ear.’ He touched his ear as if to wipe something off it.

‘Yes and I thought I heard something earlier.’ added Zelda.

‘Um, I think we might have found our Nymphs.’ Calem exclaimed.

‘What are you talking about,’ snapped Zelda,

who never liked the feeling of being enclosed, and was finding herself getting increasingly stressed by the second.

‘Oh dear,’ came a voice from behind her.

‘We have upset you.’

Zelda swung around and came face to face with a beautiful slender female with eyes so green and pointed ears. The small group stared in stunned surprise at the alluring creature and her two companions who were just as beautiful. They all had long flowing blond hair and eyes the colour of grass, each one was scantily dressed revealing their shapely figures. A pair of shimmering wings branched out from the backs of their bodies. Kadar, Teka and Calem stood with mouths wide open and eyes glazed, they had never seen such enchanting creatures before and the sight of these three mesmerised them. Zelda's nerves were not put at ease with the presence of these women as they began to walk amongst the group now paying more attention to the men, boldly touching their faces and combing their hands through their hair, flirting unashamedly with them. The men stood transfixed with gormless grins on their faces, completely enchanted by them.

‘Oh please.’ Zelda rolled her eyes upwards.

The women then turned on Zelda and pushed her towards the men.

‘What do you think you are doing?’

‘Why, Miss Zelda. We are taking you prisoners.’

The blond Nymph’s smile turned to a savage look as she ordered the men to grab the other two women. Delphine and Inna Struggled.

‘Let me go you idiot.’

Zelda's words fell on deaf ears as Calem’s hold on her was too strong and he began to drag her along the pathway while she continued to kick and scream at him, all to no avail, he was far too strong for her. Teka had pushed Inna so roughly that she stumbled and almost fell, Delphine felt so shocked that she obediently allowed Kadar to pull her along the path.

‘What the devil is going on?’ screamed Zelda.

‘I think they have put a spell on them,’ said Delphine,

who seemed less shocked than the other two, maybe it was because she had been around Cynthiana and Miska for so long. She knew the power of spells and what they could do to a person.

‘Look at their eyes it's as if they don't know us.’

The Nymphs led and the three men continued to push pull and drag the women. Inna and the others soon stopped resisting, there was no use fighting, the men were too strong and for now, there was nothing they could do but allow themselves to be the captives.

‘We will stand,’ said the one that appeared to be the leader.

‘We are here,’ she continued.

The ground began to rumble again and the bushes and tall trees started to disappear, leaving a paradise of smaller trees and flowers, pools of water, small caves and rocks. Colourful birds began to sing and standing before them a host of females wearing glorious colourful garments, beautiful radiant creatures, all with long hair, their features not quite human, their ears longer and more pointed, and their eyes more slanted and bigger. Inna had thought they would all look like her captives and was surprised to see girls with red hair, brown hair, black, as well as blond but they all had long voluptuous hair, each one was dressed scantily in bright bold colours and all had delicate iridescent wings.

The Nymphs stood smiling at their captives. The men still under some sort of spell held firmly onto the woman. Then from out of nowhere the sound of music could be heard and the Nymphs began to dance and in their hands they held long daisy chains and began to dance around the six, pushing everyone closer and closer together, wrapping the daisy chains around their captives until none of them could move. Calem and the other men struggled to free themselves, at last having come to their senses. Confused, they struggled to break free but the Nymphs had them bounded too tight, there was no escape.

The Nymphs continued to dance around the six as if they were a maypole. Tall thin vines sprung from the earth weaving itself into a prison around its captives securely trapping them. Satisfied with their work, the Nymphs stopped dancing, the music ceased and the daisy chain ropes fell away from their prisoners leaving them free within the jail. The enchanting creatures admired their work. Then a gentle fluttering sound began as the Nymphs began to take to the sky and vanish out of sight, leaving the group stunned by the events, and unable to believe how easy their capture had been on behalf of these delicate looking creatures. They stood in silence for a moment. Zelda was the first one to let rip, by slapping Calem on the arm.

‘Ow what's that for?’

‘That's for pushing and dragging me to this place.’

‘We could not help it; they put a spell on us.’

‘You should have been more aware and protected yourself,’

Clearly Zelda was not amused or in the mood to be forgiving.

‘Now what are we supposed to do?’

She dramatically threw her hands in the air, Calem rolled his eyes. Inna truly loved Zelda but she sure did have a flare for the theatrical. There was no sign of the Nymphs it was obvious they had gone, and it did not look like they were coming back. Calem began shaking the prison structure but to no avail, Kadar and Teka began to help him, after all it was only made of branches, they tried cutting it, but that didn't work, they tried putting a flame to it, and that did nothing.

This was not good thought Inna, here we are trapped, time running out and no idea how we are going to get the word. She could sense the frustration amongst everyone rising as the light began to fade meaning another day was slipping away from them. Inna could not help but wonder if the veil of blindness was holding, she hoped with all of her heart that Lithmore and all her people were being kept safe from the dreaded Adreds.

There was so much chatter going on inside the small jail, Inna was finding it hard to think and found herself wishing just for a moment, everyone would just shut up.

‘I agree,’ came a voice.

Inna snapped her head around and came face to face with a small wizened old woman with pointy ears and shaggy brown hair with streaks of white in it. Her eyes were green like the colour of frogs with a hint of mischief in them and attached to her back were two golden wings. The others were so busy talking amongst themselves they hadn’t even noticed her.

‘Shall we get them to shut up?’ The old woman winked.

Inna immediately felt she could trust this stranger. She nodded her head in answer to the old woman.

‘BE QUIET.’

The voice was loud and commanding, everyone froze, Inna burst out laughing as they all looked like naughty children. They turned their attention to where the voice came from to see the small woman standing before them.

‘That's better, I like quiet, peace and quiet, that is what I like.’

She stood and observed each of the prisoners one by one, taking her time and when she was done she said.

'Right it's time to get rid of these walls,' and within an instance the prison walls vanished leaving the captives free. Inna's sigh of relief did not go unnoticed. The old woman pointed at Inna,

'You, dear heart, - you are the chosen one.'

The old women was looking directly at Inna. What does she mean thought Inna, the chosen one, but before she could ask, the old women went on.

'You have come for the word, have you not?'

They all nodded in unison. Surely this was not the Key Nymph.

'In answer to your unspoken question,- I am she.'

Everyone was flabbergasted. The Key Nymph laughed at their shallowness. They had expected her to be as beautiful and youthful as the other Nymphs. But it was Inna who saw her beauty, the real beauty of the Key Nymph, because she saw kindness and generosity, humour and laughter, she felt joy, and healing with this woman, she felt as if she were in the presence of someone very, very special, yes, she appeared old and had lines on her face, and wrinkled hands and white streaks in her hair but to Inna she was more beautiful than all the others because her beauty came from within and spoke through her eyes that were now smiling straight at Inna.

'Come girl, walk with me and you can tell me of your troubles and what we might do to help you.'

The old women extended her hand to Inna and led her away from the others who seemed unconcerned to see Inna go off with the old Nymph.

'Have we all been charmed into thinking she is ok do you think?' Teka asked nervously.

'No, -Did you not see Inna's face? She has total trust in that old women.'

Zelda was smiling for the first time in what seemed like ages.

The two strangers walked silently for a while yet Inna felt comfortable in the presence of this old Nymph a similar feeling she had when she had been in the company of her Grandmother. Intuitively she sensed a powerful bond between them.

'By the way, my name is Harmeni.'

What a pretty name, thought Inna.

The old Nymph stopped walking and turned to Inna, for a moment she seemed to be reading the young girls face searching for answers to something.

'Now tell me child. What brings you here? Oh I know what you want and why but what I want to know is how it all began and why. Why is it you are so young to be the chosen one?'

Inna thought for a moment then decided she should start at the beginning with the passing of her Grandmother and because her mother had died when she was an infant, she had been thrown into the role of Queen of Lithmore and Keeper of the Living Stone, the latter role bestowed on all female rulers of Lithmore.

'The Living Stone is the most powerful healing stone in all the known world with the ability, to cure even the most deadly of sicknesses, Many people come in need of the Living Stone's powers and with them they bring much revenue to the city which makes us a very wealthy powerful nation.' Inna was finding it very easy opening up to Hermini who had plonked herself on the ground and was listening intently to what Inna was saying.

'Cynthiana,' she continued, 'has stolen the stone to weaken the city so that she can send her monsters in to seize Lithmore, it is not the city alone she wants but the whole of the Lithmorian region as it is believed the area is full of gold mines and she intends to lay claim to it all. Cynthiana and her sidekick Miska, stole the stone and then set about enticing people away from Lithmore to bathe in the lake of prespa which supposedly had healing powers but Delphine, Cynthiana's mother, who, by the way, she tried to murder, suspected it was just a spell and would soon wear off but by then she would have managed to have enticed many people away from Lithmore leaving the city vulnerable so that her army could march in. Well that was her plan, until she decided to awake the Adreds. In the meantime, once the Living Stone had been stolen I discovered that my life force was connected to the stone, you see as the Keeper it is my job to sing to the stone daily, it is what feeds it and gives it life force but until it was stolen I did not know it worked both ways and my life depends on connecting to the stone, so of course we have to find it. My life was draining away from me then we came across the Children of Vision who helped me to astral project to the stone. They saved my life and then they told us we must find you and that we have a much bigger mission than just finding the stone, we have to rid the earth of the Adreds.'

The old Nymph had remained silent, nodding and shaking her head from time to time but Inna could see, she was clearly excited at the mention of the Children of Vision.

'They told you to come and find me.'

'Yes, they said it was you and only you that could give us the word.'

'Was it now? Well, I am delighted at that so I am, delighted and pleased.'

And for the first time Inna could see a youthfulness on Harmeni's face.

'And I suppose they warned you about our antics,' the old women's eyes danced with mischief.

Inna's cheeks flushed slightly embarrassed.

'Well, yes, they might have said something.'

Harmeni laughed out loud.

'Well now you have told me what has led you here, now I want to know a little about you. Tell me a little about your parents.' The old women instantly saw a change in Inna's eyes.

'I never knew my parents, they both died when I was just a few days old.'

'Oh, I am so sorry my dear,'

'I was just a baby when they were killed, apparently they had gone to one of the islands to bring an infant back to the stone for healing and sadly got caught in a freak storm, the small boat they were in got smashed against the rocks and all three died. My Grandmother raised me and now she is gone I am left as ruler and keeper.'

Inna proudly held herself erect.

'My proper title is Queen Inna Marlarna Alannis. Keeper of the Living Stone.' She gave a little curtsey.

'That's a big title for someone so young,' the old Nymph was full of compassion for her new young friend.

'I think you must be a very special soul, to have come into this life and taken on so much responsibility and quite rightly I believe you are a pure soul, one who can take the word and rid the awful Adreds once and for all. Know this dear heart, it only takes one Adred to hear the word and all the others will automatically be destroyed but be warned, you can only ever use the word once, so you can never repeat it to anyone until you are ready to use it. If you succeed, it will turn the Adreds hearts to stone taking their breath away, they will disintegrate into dust, and the earth will be rid of them forever.

The old Nymph stood up and for a moment studied Inna who was feeling slightly nervous unsure of what was about to happen.

‘Come closer now dear heart, it's time to receive the word, stand in front of me, I will not speak it, but breathe it into your ear you will take it in and keep it within until you need it. You will hear it as soon as you receive it, but let me remind you. You must not voice it until you need it. Do you understand?’

Inna nodded, although she felt strangely apprehensive as the old woman began to lean forward and breathed out into her ear, she heard the rush of air and the sound of a word, for an instance she felt her heart had turned to stone and a chill ran down her spine.

‘Breathe child.’

Inna began to take deep breaths. It was done, she had indeed received the secret word.

CHAPTER SIXTEEN

Cynthiana paced the large hall, her hands behind her back, her head held high with her chin sticking firmly out, she was deep in thought. The guards around the great hall stood to attention hardly daring to breathe for fear of drawing attention to themselves. They could see that Cynthiana was not happy and there were always consequences when their Queen was not happy and they were right, she was most displeased, she had been down to visit the stone and, to her surprise, it was beaming, radiating colours all around the cave creating a beacon of light. It was as though it had been given new life, but how could that be, thought Cynthiana, that could only happen with the connection of Inna and from what she had last seen Inna was too weak to do anything let alone come here, break into the palace, and find her way to the stone. No this was odd, very odd. Cynthiana shook her head. Something was not right here.

She had not wanted anyone else other than Miska and herself knowing about the stone or its whereabouts but now she felt it was important to place a twenty four hour guard on it. She needed to monitor it.

*****

Cynthiana stopped pacing and turned to one of the guards. A guard should not be fearful, the young man knew this but he had seen so many bad things happen that he knew for certain having the attention of Cynthiana was not a good thing.

'You.' She pointed at him; his heart began to race and pound within his chest.

'Step forward.'

Bravely he took one step forward. She left him standing there and moved around the hall, stopping once again in front of another young guard. She could see his face drain of all colour and wickedly smiled to herself in the knowledge that she had so much power.

'You, step forward.'

Without hesitation the young guard did as instructed.

'Right you two men follow me, the rest of you are dismissed.'

Without question they fell in step behind her, their eyes met briefly questioningly, neither one knowing the answer of what lay ahead of them. Cynthiana led them out of the hall down the corridors then without warning just stopped and swung around facing the two young men.

'What you are about to see and do, you must never reveal to another living soul. Your lives depend on it. Do you understand me?' They both nodded their heads nervously.

'Do you understand me?' she shrieked.

'Yes, yes your Majesty,' they both stammered.

'Good, that's better,'

and with that said she turned and faced the wall. With a slight smirk spread across her face she placed her hand onto one of the stones, to the surprise of the two young men the stone wall opened up like a door, and they were ushered through. They found themselves in a narrow corridor lit by lanterns, Cynthiana did not speak but continued to walk along the corridor.

'Keep up,' she called to them as she speedily made her way along the narrow path.

It appeared to the two guards that they were going down deep below the ground; they could smell the dampness of earth and the staleness of the air. Rocks began to appear and they had to negotiate around them, they soon arrived at the entrance to a large cave, they could see a large pool of water the colour of turquoise the whole place appeared to be full of light and colour; the atmosphere here seemed to instantly put the young guards at ease it was so beautiful and welcoming. In the distance they noticed a large stone; it seemed to be pulsating energy from it. Both young men seemed instantly in awe of their surroundings, they were extremely curious of the big stone.

'You two are to remain down here and guard that stone. Food and supplies will be brought to you. One of you is to remain awake at all times. You will report only to myself or Miska, anything that happens here. I will repeat what I said earlier you are to speak of this to no one,- ever. Do you understand?'

'Yes, your Majesty,' they replied in unison.

Contented that they understood what she wanted from them she turned and made her exit leaving the two young guards feeling a little bewildered but quite liking the task they had been given.

*****

'Well have you found out where that wretched girl and her herd of followers are?'

Cynthiana was sitting with her feet up in her chambers looking directly at Miska, who appeared to be increasingly more troubled and frightened by her mistress. Yes she had managed to discover where they were but why they were there, she did not know, what she did know was that by divulging the information to Cynthiana it was going to send her into a stinking rage.

'Well, where are they?' Cynthiana was in no mood to be bamboozled.

Miska released a heavy sigh.

'It appears that Inna and the others have gone in search of the Key Nymph but for what reason I don't know.'

Confused by this information Cynthiana decided they must be trying to find a way into Maro to retrieve the stone. There was no way, she thought, they could know about the Adreds, of that she was certain. Feeling contented with her reasoning she determined not to give it another thought, for the moment anyway, she had much more important things on her mind, she was becoming increasingly concerned not to have received any reports from the Adreds, she had thought that by now they would have managed to have taken Lithmore. She needed to send Miska back to her little pot of water to add her splash of magic to see what was going on.

Miska was feeling quite happy as she waddled along the corridors beside her mistress towards her little hovel. Cynthiana had decided to join her so that she could see for herself what was going on with Inna and her little gang. Miska was pleased Cynthiana was being congenial towards her for once, it made a nice change from the recent foul mood she had been in during the past few days. Sadly for Miska that was all about to change.

As they both gazed into the pot, they could see the Adreds flying around where Lithmore should be but there was no sign of a city, no buildings, nothing. How could that be? Both women looked at each other, completely puzzled.

'It's as though Lithmore has vanished.' screamed Cynthiana.

'Or hidden.' suggested Miska.

'What do you mean?'

‘Have you ever heard of a wall of blindness?’

‘No I haven't what is it?’ spat Cynthiana

‘Well, it is difficult to do, but I think they have been doing it to hide themselves from us. that is why it has been so difficult to track them. A wall of blindness takes various forms and has varying strengths, If they have managed to put a wall of blindness up around Lithmore it must have taken some doing.’ There was a trace of admiration in Miska's voice,

‘Yes, yes, but what is it.’

‘It’s a wall of energy that puts a shield up so you cannot see what is truly there. The Adreds are flying around the city but they don't know it, because they can't see it.’

‘How ingenious, now, how do we destroy it?’

Miska could not help but release a small giggle.

‘Do you remember the spell we used to change the lake into healing waters? Well it is a little like that one, but first you must recall one of the Adreds back here so that she can take it back and disperse it over the area of Lithmore. Once she has the spell on her, all she has to do is return to the area of Lithmore and as soon as she flies into wall of blindness the city will be revealed’

‘Excellent.’

Cynthiana was amazed at how easy this all seemed.

‘Now all we need to do is get one of those monsters back here.’

‘Oh that's easy enough, see this band on my wrist, it is connected to all of the Adreds. Before I awoke them, I placed a collar around every one of their necks and this device on my wrist controls each and every one of them. All I have to do is send a signal to one of them and they will come. Ingenious don't you think?

Miska had to agree it was quite brilliant. They decided they had no time to lose. Cynthiana set about calling one of the Adreds back to Maro while Miska busily set to work conjuring up the spell to disperse the wall of blindness. Both women were in uncommonly good moods for a change.

Remembering the guards and knowing it was going to be some time before the Adred arrived, Cynthiana decided it was time to pay a visit down to the cave for her first report. She would take Miska as the men would need feeding and she had no intention of carrying anything. Off they set down the small pathway, Cynthiana floated along, poor Miska struggling with a basket strapped to her back waddling behind, huffing and puffing from the load she was carrying.

Eventually they arrived at the cave to be greeted by two very excited young guards. The cave appeared even brighter than before. Both the men began to speak at the same time so quickly and excitedly that Cynthiana could not understand either of them.

'Stop, talking,' she held her hand up to silence them.

Both men stood to attention in front of her.

'Right, take a deep breath, now you,' pointing to the first guard.

'You speak, what has happened here?'

'We could not believe it your Majesty; we could not believe our eyes.'

'What, what did you see?'

'It was amazing.' jumped in the second guard.

'I am so going to strike someone in a minute if you don't tell me what has happened here.'

Cynthiana glared from one to the other. The guards stood rigid barely daring to breathe. The first guard inhaled deeply then began to tell Cynthiana what they had seen.

'We had both been sitting over there. Nothing was happening except the stone appeared to be losing its energy. The cave was becoming dimmer the colours in here were more muted.'

'It did not feel so nice in here,' added the second guard.

'That's right, it began to feel colder and,' the young guard paused and hung his head down embarrassed.

'What, what?'

'We began to feel very sad.'

'Then what?' oblivious to the guards feelings, Cynthiana was keen for the guard to get on with his story.

'Then all of a sudden, this girl appears.'

'Girl, what girl, what did she look like, where did she come from?'

'Well that's just it. We don't know where she came from, she just appeared.'

The two young men looked at each other.

'She was very beautiful.'

'Then what?'

Cynthiana, eager to learn more.

'Well we tried to get her attention, we went up to her but she ignored us, she seemed to be communing with the stone. We grabbed her but our hands went right through her, there was nothing to grab.'

The young man's eyes were as big as saucers.

'It was as if she were a ghost, then she began to sing and the singing filled the cave it was so delightful and colours began to swirl around, the most beautiful colours you ever did see, and the stone began to pulsate light, it was the most captivating scene. Then as quickly as she came she was gone. The only change was the stone seemed to have been restored somehow.'

Cynthiana and Miska looked at one another. Had Inna transported they wondered, although it did not seem likely if the guards had tried to touch her. Cynthiana knew she should be outraged by these events but she was strangely intrigued by what had occurred, there was nothing she could do about it at the moment but she knew she would have to deal with it. If Inna had managed in some way to come to the cave to connect to the Living Stone she had obviously done it before and would do it again, she must set a trap but first, and more importantly, she must insure the fall of Lithmore.

Cynthiana and Miska left the two young guards having praised them for their work and ordering them to continue with their observations and instead of being frighten or apprehensive they found that they were delighted to be remaining in the cave, they loved the energy that surrounded them, and somehow it made them feel safe and unafraid.

On the journey back to the palace Cynthiana and Miska discussed Inna at great length. Cynthiana was determined to capture Lithmore's Queen and keep her and the Living Stone for her own purpose. It seemed clear that Inna was determined to get the stone back, however Cynthiana felt convinced Inna or the people of Lithmore were unaware of their forthcoming attack. Cynthiana knew that Lithmore had lain itself vulnerable by sending its army to retrieve the stone. All was going well she thought. Perhaps, in hindsight, she should have had the Adreds deal with the Lithmorian army before sending them to attack Lithmore, but no matter, there would be plenty of time before they reached Maro.

Yes, thought Cynthiana all is going well.

Later as darkness fell the Adred appeared. Miska had conjured up everything that was needed and gave it to Cynthiana who ceremoniously waved its contents over the Adred. For such a fierce and horrid creature it seemed to take great delight in Cynthiana's company and uncharacteristically for Cynthiana she appeared warm and gentle to the horrid vile creature. However no time was wasted and soon the Adred was on her way back to Lithmore to disperse the wall of blindness.

Cynthiana could sleep well tonight believing that she would soon have control over the whole of the Lithmorian region and its people, well those that survived, she laughed, a smug and nasty little laugh to herself as she pulled her feather blanket up beneath her chin. In no time Miska would lead her to the gold mines and then she would be the richest being in the entire world. As she lay in her bed thinking of these thoughts a slight pang of guilt passed through her, she had been pretty rotten to Miska of late, after all, none of these things would have been possible without her at her side.

Yawning, she determined to be nicer to her little friend. The dynamics between them had changed much recently considering at one time Miska called all the shots. Cynthiana would do well to remember that Miska had been responsible for bringing her into this world in a way, she had taught her everything she knew and had encouraged and developed her skills until she had become more powerful than Miska, or was she? Her briefly calmed thoughts now turned more sinister. What if Miska was just play acting? What if she had more powers of magic that she had not yet divulged? What if, when Lithmore has been captured and the gold found, Miska turns on her, and betrays her. Cynthiana's head was now spinning with what ifs. One thing was for sure, while she had control over the Adreds no one could touch her and with that thought in her head she drifted off to sleep.

CHAPTER SEVENTEEN

Zelda was the first one to spot Inna returning to them and sprang to her feet to greet her.

'Where is the key Nymph?'

'She said, to say goodbye, but she had to go.' Inna seemed relaxed, that was good, thought Zelda.

'Well,' Teka asked eagerly.

'Did she give you the word?'

'She did.'

'Well what is it?'

'You know perfectly well I cannot repeat it, so don't ask.'

Teka looked disappointed.

'Well our task here is done and we must return to Lithmore.'

Calem felt unsure of what lay ahead of them but he knew they had no time to lose. Had the veil of blindness held, or had it fallen, was the city of Lithmore already under attack if so would they be in time to save them. Everyone could see Calem's concern and felt his anxiety.

'It would just be too awful to return too late.' said Zelda.

'We must not think that way.' Inna chastised her.

For a moment everyone stood still, not saying a word, almost afraid to speak or move. The thought of coming face to face with an Adred was more than any of them could bear. Each one of them in their own right were brave souls and so far during their journey they had proved that they could overcome most things but just in this moment they knew they were returning to face the Adreds and only a fool or a madman would be free of fear.

They huddled together, it was becoming second nature to them all now, Calem asked very quietly and softly if everyone was ready, everyone nodded. and their short powerful journey back to Lithmore began.

They arrived just inside the gates of Lithmore to a stampede of people running and screaming towards them. There was chaos and fires burning and a noise none of them had heard before. People scattered into buildings in an attempt to escape but Inna and the rest just stood there looking towards the gate where they could see fire shooting up over the walls. There was no doubt in their minds that the Adreds where on the other side and there was no time to think or prepare, the time was now to put a stop to them, everyone turned to Inna. Calem was drained of colour, convinced that they were up against an impossible task. he feared for Inna's life, who was he kidding he was afraid for all of them. the screeching alone sent terror to the very core of his being.

'What do we do,' screamed Zelda,

'There is no way we are going to be able to put a stop to them.'

Just then a large head appeared, the Adreds had broken the gates down and now they were stomping through. Hugh, terrifying creatures, first the head of one, then another appeared. They witnessed a citizen desperately trying to get out of reach of one of them, only to be scooped up and tossed into the air. They all watched in horror as the creature caught the poor man in its mouth and began to devour him. Dalphine already faint with fear, felt sick to her stomach but there is no time for fainting or for being sick.

‘They have got to see me before I shout the word or it will not work. I need to get higher so that I can call to them.’ Instructed Inna.

The last thing Delphine wanted to attract was the predators gaze upon herself. Calem scanned the area for a possible platform for Inna.

‘This way, come on everyone, we need to get over to that tower, we can climb up there hopefully the wall will protect us, Inna you can call through that window.’

A third Adred appeared and there were more citizens that found themselves victims of these monsters. Calem, Inna, Teka, Zelda, Kadar and Delphine began to make their way to the tower ducking and diving to avoid being seen. With hearts racing and fear thundering through their veins they all ran towards the tower and almost managed to make it to cover safely amidst the piercing screams of those poor citizens that did not when Delphine tripped and stumbled to the ground she landed with a thud. Everyone froze, they were so close to cover but still so exposed out in the open.

Kadar rushed to Delphines side and scooped her up in his strong arms.

‘Go, I'll take care of her.’ Kadar voice was commanding.

No one wanted to leave them, Kadar could see the concern in their faces.

‘Go, go, I'll take care of her, you do what you need to do.’

Terrified at what may happen to them but knowing they had no choice Inna, Calem Teka and Zelda turned to continue making their way to the tower, none of them dare look back for fear the screams they heard belonged to Kadar and Delphine.

Having managed to reach the tower building they all collapsed against the wall to regain their breath they had made it to the tower. Instinctively Inna grabbed her crystal around her neck and called her Grandmother to her for strength.

'Go to the roof top.' Inna could have sworn she heard her Grandmothers voice.

'Go to the roof top.' She heard the voice again.

Inna did not know why she needed to be high off the ground in order to face the Adreds but every core of her being told her that was the thing she had to do. She knew she had to be looking down at them when she got their attention.

'Come on this way,' ordered Calem.

'No, we have to go to the roof top.'

'But you will be exposed there.' Calem protested.

'I know but that is where I have to be.'

They had all learned to trust Inna's instincts by now and although it was against Calem's better judgment he nodded his head in agreement. They would need to take a different flight of steps to reach the roof. Once they all had chance to catch their breaths they began to make their way along the corridors to the stairway leading up to the roof. At all times they continued to hear the sound of the Adreds it seemed there were more and more of them entering the city.

After several minutes the four of them managed to make it to the top of the roof. Looking up and around cautious of being spotted in such an open space they crept to the edge of the roof to see below. From their viewpoint Inna could see most of Lithmore. Adreds were destroying buildings, her beautiful city was being destroyed by these monsters. How was she ever going to stop them. For a moment she felt completely overwhelmed and beaten. Who was she kidding what was one word going to do. against such power. they were all doomed.

‘Go to the statue of the falcon.’ Again, Inna could hear her Grandmother's voice.

Go to the statue of the falcon, she repeated to herself. looking around the roof top she could see several statues of various creatures standing on the edge of the roof top overlooking the city. Finally she spotted the falcon, motioning to the others she pointed to the statue. warily they made their way over to the bird.

‘Now what?’

Calem, who was never going to get used to taking instructions from anyone other than himself fixed his eyes on Inna. She looked absolutely terrified how on earth was she going to manage to defeat these monsters. But instead of answering him she turned to the falcon statue and placed her hands upon it. To everyone's astonishment the stone bird began to move. They all jumped back in retreat except Inna, who just smiled, the falcon turned his head and gently cooed, he motioned his head towards his back.

‘He wants you to get on his back’ Zelda cried.

‘Wow I think you are right.’ said Inna

‘I think he is going to fly you down to the Adreds. ‘ Calem was looking up at the large bird when he was speaking and to his surprise saw the bird nod his head.

‘Quick Inna get on him. We will get the Adreds attention.’

Calem and Teka helped Inna onto the falcon, then made it their business to get the attention of the Adreds. Grabbing his catapult Teka aimed at one of the wretched creatures below and took aim, then began shooting small stones carefully aimed at the Adred’s head. the Adred let out a sharp screech and appeared a little confused then Calem began to shout and wave his arms in the air attracting the Adreds attention. She sees him and with one leap takes to the air. The falcons wings begin to flap and within seconds Inna is flying through the air first circling in the sky. The attacked Adred sees the falcon and ignores Calem and begins to take chase after the bird and Inna. The other Adreds on the ground appear oblivious to what is going on more interested in continuing with their destruction on the ground.

The falcon is much faster than the Adred who is furiously flapping her wings in an attempt to catch up with the bird. she attempts to shoot fire through the air at her target but they are just out of reach of her. Inna is holding on for dear life. No time for fear, no time for any emotion, her only thought now is to destroy the Adreds.

Calem, Zelda, and Teka watch from the roof top with their hearts in their mouths terrified that Inna will not survive this battle. Calem looks to the ground and notices another of the Adreds taking to the sky's she has seen what is happening. more Adreds are starting to pay attention to what is going on and another one takes off but before either one of them can reach their companion the falcon suddenly turns towards the Adred face on and hovers in the sky, the Adred continues towards both the falcon and Inna with the taste of victory in her mouth.

A strong wind begins to blow against Inna's back becoming so powerful Inna fears she will lose her grip and fall to the earth before she has a chance to complete her mission. She holds tighter as the wind gets louder and stronger she can see the Adred trying to get closer to them but the wind is too powerful and she is unable to move forward. It is then that Inna knows it is now that she must release the WORD. She cries out with all the power she can muster. from the depth of her being.

'LU UM MU SHA OM' The words come out of her mouth like thunder and are carried out over the wind to the ears of the angry Adred, immediately her wings stop flapping. For a brief moment there is stillness, then an explosion and she is no more, the other two Adreds meet the same fate. The sudden wind ceases, gone as quick as it came, leaving the sky calm once more. Inna cannot believe her eyes. Could they really have done it, could they really have gotten rid of the dreaded Adreds. She looks to the earth and as the falcon flies over the city she can see that it is true every single Adred has gone, erased from the earth forever.

Gently the falcon returns to the roof top. Greeted by smiles. Teka is jumping for joy and even Calem usually restrained grabs Zelda and swings her around pulling her closer and closer until without knowing how they got there found themselves in a deep and passionate kiss.

'Uh um. would someone mind helping me down.' Inna laughs. Feeling absolutely exhilarated by her experience.

Calem and Zelda break away from their kiss slightly red faced feeling embarrassed that the excitement of the moment had let their guards down.

'Oh please you two when are you going to admit you are made for each other.' Teka gently helps Inna to the ground.

'It's true, you are.' agreed Inna.

'You are made for each other, so when are you going to stop fighting it, and start owning it.' Inna laughed again.

Both Calem and Zelda coyly looked at each other, it was true they had feelings for each other, It did seem rather silly that they kept fighting it. Calem gently grabbed Zelda's hand and again pulled her to him.

'What do say miss Zelda should we make a team?'

Zelda just smiled and nodded her head to which Calem responded with another kiss.

'Oh my, what about Delphine and Kadar, we must go and see if we can find them.'

'What about him.' Teka was pointing to the falcon.

'Oh.' Inna turned to her comrade.

'How can I thank you. for all that you have done. Without you, we would not have been able to beat the Adreds. I will be eternally grateful to you. The falcon cooed again and gently nudged his head against Inna's then straightened himself up and turned back into stone.

'Oh no, I can't bear to think that he has done so much for us and now, his reward is that he remains as stone forever.'

As happy as Inna had felt a few moments ago, now she felt tears slipping down her face for the loss of her brave new friend. Kissing the stone falcon. she turned to the others.

'Well this has been a great victory but we still have yet another battle to win if we are to get the Living Stone back to its rightful place. But for now we need to find Delphine and Kadar and make sure Hiliron is ok.

To the mass relief of everyone Delphine and Kadar were found safe they had managed to escape the Adreds. Delphine had broken her arm and twisted her ankle in the fall but was in high spirits when she saw that everyone was safe. The citizens of Lithmore were starting to come out into the streets having heard the sounds of cheers from those that were caught outside and had survived. People began to dance for joy and celebration began to break out amongst the survivors and people rushed to the aid of those that needed it. How many had been taken she wondered but looking around now she thought not as many as she had first feared. they must have gotten here just in time. The veil of blindness must have just broken down just before their return, that was why the Adreds were still outside. What did it matter if a few buildings were destroyed they could be rebuilt. it was the people that mattered.

As it turned out in the end only five people had lost their lives, several had been injured through falling debris or injured in their attempts to escape but because most people were hidden away inside the buildings the majority remained safe. The only people that had been out in the streets were the males that had took it upon themselves to keep a look out and to monitor that the veil of blindness held firm. Brave men, Inna knew that they were not trained to fight, these were men of trade. Still thought Inna five men was five men too many but there were ten thousand people hidden within the walls of Lithmore and in that moment Inna felt truly humbled knowing that they could all sleep safely in their beds tonight.

The excitement of defeating the Adreds was electrifying. Hiliron had spotted the returning hero's coming across the courtyard and called to Abron before running down the stone steps to greet them. All protocol forgotten as he raced towards Inna with outstretched arms.

'Inna my dear, dear, girl. You did it, you have saved us all. '

Hiliron held her close to him but his brief moment of joy turned to anxiousness as he felt the lack of energy within Inna, he pulled her away from him so that he could study her face, he could see she was forcing a smile but her face was very pale, and she was not standing in her normal erect stance.

'Come my dear, we need to get you rested.'

Everyone was so excited that they seemed oblivious to the conversation going on between Hiliron and Inna.

'You need to connect to the stone?'

Inna looked at Hiliron with fear and anxiety in her eyes.

'What's wrong my dear? why do you look so fearful?'

At that moment Inna's knees began to give way attracting everyone's attention, she grabbed onto Hiliron's hands.

'Save me, Hiliron, - I don't think I can help myself anymore.'

And before she could say another word she collapsed into his arms. the sound of gasps could be heard. Calem and Teka rushed to Hiliron's side and gently took Inna from him then moved swiftly up the steps and down the corridors and through into her chambers. They were quickly followed by Hiliron, Abron, and Zelda who for once had not spoken a word since Inna collapsed. Kadar followed at the back carrying Delphine. All were aware that Inna was desperate to connect to the Living Stone and although in the past she had been able to astral travel they all feared that she was now to weak.

As Calem and Teka lay her gently onto the bed they could all see the severity of the situation.

'We have to take her to the stone, now, we have no more time, no more choices.'

As Teka spoke, his voice was full of fear. His looked around the chamber at the others, pleading looking for support. Hiliron was sure the army would be close to Maro and the attack would be imminent, But he too was aware that it was imperative that Inna be reunited with the stone as soon as possible.

'We are pretty sure Cynthiana has the stone hidden in a cave deep under the palace, we know we can reach it by two ways, the first would take too much time to reach it and the second, is dangerous and only Delphine knows the secret passage.'

'Then I will show you how to find it.' Delphine was now standing.

'But your injured.' exclaimed Zelda.

'We can't let that get in the way. Abron can fix me up with whatever he does, the arms hurting like a bald faced hornet but it will pass.'

'There is no need I know the passages as well as you do I will take them.’ Kadar insisted.

‘No, you don't know where this one is.’

Delphine, felt a little guilty that she had never told Kadar where the entrance to the caves could be found but then she never dreamt there would be any need to.

‘We haven't got time to debate this. If you know how to reach the stone you must come with us. Look, her breathing is becoming more and more shallow.’

Calem's observation of Inna was frighteningly accurate. She was dying in front of them. they had no time to waste. It was imperative they got her to the stone and fast.

CHAPTER EIGHTEEN

'Oh no, no, no, no, this can't be.'

Miska began jumping up and down, screaming, frustration and anger consuming her,

looking into her little pot she had just witnessed the destruction of the Adreds. This was terrible how were they going to take Lithmore now and worse still the Lithmorian army was only a few miles away from Maro. Cynthiana's insistence in using the Adreds had ruined her plans she was never going to get to the gold mines at this rate. Why had she not insisted they hold back and allow Lithmore to fall into decline then go in with their army quietly, unexpectedly and take Lithmore. What a fool she had been giving Cynthiana so much power. The whole purpose of stealing the Living Stone was to draw away the many travellers that visited Lithmore to weaken their trade and therefore make the city more vulnerable. But no, thought Miska, Cynthiana insisted on doing it her way and now all we have is a mess.

At that moment her thoughts are disturbed by the door bursting open, a breathless Cynthiana stands before her. For a brief moment they both look at each other, neither one knowing what the other is going to do, or say. Miska does not feel like being sub servant today .

'Inna has destroyed the Adreds.' Miska's eyes firmly fix on Cynthiana, waiting for her explosive reaction but to Miska's surprise there is none.

'I know, well, I did not know for sure, but I knew they were gone, I could feel it. how strange is that Miska I felt them die.'

Cynthiana looked defeated.

‘What are we going to do Miska?’

Cynthiana seemed lost and for the first time in a very long time she seemed to be turning to her old friend and companion for help. Perhaps, thought Miska, her young Queen might listen a little more intently to her advice in the future. Cynthiana threw her arms around her little friend and while Miska's gently patted the young girls back to console her, her mind was busy planning their next move.

‘Well one thing is for sure.’ Miska gently pushed Cynthiana away from her.

‘Inna will be eager to retrieve the stone now that they have secured Lithmore.’

‘No, no she can't. what can we do?’

Cynthiana appeared to have lost all confidence in herself, Miska could see that she was still very much a child at heart and that all her fears and concerns that Cynthiana had become too powerful, were silly worries on her part. Miska thought for a moment, she would have to take charge if they were to stand a chance of victory over this troublesome Inna and her merry little gang of helpers. There was no way that she was going to lose the chance of possessing the gold mines but in order to succeed they were going to have to get rid of Inna and her little band of helpers permanently.

‘It's bad, your Majesty, I won't lie to you. but it is nothing we can't solve.’

Cynthiana gave a little sigh of relief.

‘First we must ensure that the Lithmorian army does not reach here. Our army is big and strong enough to ward them off. but we must keep enough good men here in case we need them. The second thing we must do is destroy the stone.’

Cynthiana inhaled a sharp intake of breath at the mention of destroying the stone. In some strange way she had become strangely attached and had no wish to destroy it.

'Must we.' Cynthiana voice was almost whiny.

'By destroying the stone we will be destroying Inna.'

It was all starting to make sense now, of course. If there is no stone there will be no Inna.

No Inna no Queen of Lithmore. It was a shame, thought Cynthiana, but yes, the stone must be destroyed. Miska believed it would not be an easy task to extinguish the stone and began churning her jaw in a chewing motion while she gave it some thought. It was going to take magic and lots of it, she decided.

It's an odd thing dynamics between two people how quickly things can change. For many years Miska ruled everything not that anyone knew it, the older Cynthiana got the more power Miska gave her, the dynamics sifted between them and Cynthiana became the stronger more controlling one and for a while Miska although always loving Cynthiana felt perhaps she had given Cynthiana too much power, certainly of late she had not appreciated the violent outburst towards herself and had begun to wonder if Cynthiana was only concerned with seizing the mines and Lithmore for herself, but today her fears had been alleviated for the moment at least that Cynthiana still needed her but perhaps she would take advantage of this time and ensure that Cynthiana maintain a little more respect for her in the future.

Dam and blast, thought Cynthiana She had not meant to be so weak and vulnerable, she had been stupid to allow Miska to see her fears. Losing the Adreds had come as a big shock to her, not for one moment did she believe Inna capable of destroying them, now her plans were well and truly ruined, She did not mind Miska enjoying the spoils of the mines but she was determined it was she who would own them and it would be she who ruled Lithmore. Although she knew she owed much to Miska there was a part of Cynthiana that screamed, do not trust her.

Once again the dark thoughts began to creep in 'was she just being used' for the first time in her life she felt what it must feel like to be a puppet, she could not stop the questions spinning around in her head, questions like, had she ever had an original thought of her own that was not planted by Miska. After all it was Miska who taught her everything, to hate her parents. Would she have killed her own father had it not been for the influence of Miska or was she really that rotten. None of it seemed to matter anymore, she thought, this is now and I want Lithmore for myself, not for Miska, I want the mines, the lands, the power, and I want Miska put back in her place. Cynthiana had magic of her own and although she was willing to learn what Magic Miska intended to use to get rid of Inna she intended to conjure up some magic of her own.

Maro's army was sent out to meet the Lithmorian army. They had intended to lay a trap for the soldiers but were too late, word had arrived that they were closer than they had thought. The army had been spotted on the plains, a large flat wasteland outside Maro.

‘We must separate the land between us.’ instructed Miska.

‘Can we do that?’

‘We can and it will give us time.’ Miska seemed sure of her words.

‘For us to succeed we need to be on the plains and it will take both of us to conjure up enough power to separate the earth.’

‘Then we must hurry.’

The fastest and fittest horses were got ready and the two women along with a band of soldiers went racing out of the palace heading towards the plains. The women rode like expert horseman, Miska who had been lifted upon her steed rode surprisingly well for a little fat dwarf the stirrups had been adjusted for her very short legs. Her cloak flapped around from the speed of her white horse as she fell in behind Cynthiana's black stallion, a majestic powerful beast that led the small party through the forest onto the plains. Within a short time they had met up with Maro's army passing them and going on ahead it was then they could see in the distance the cloud of dust in the air looking like mountains heading towards them. There was no doubt. It was the Lithmorian army. They brought their horses to a halt.

'We have to stop them now they are too close.' called Miska.

Cynthiana dismounted her horse, full of determination. She stood facing the oncoming army. Miska remained on her horse but pulled up besides Cynthiana.

'Remember to cover your face.'

Miska remarked as she pulled a rag out and placed it around her mouth. Cynthiana did as she was instructed. Then without any further words both women began to chant. Cynthiana's arms raised to the sky and Miska's attentions faced down to the earth. The day had been warm suddenly began to chill, the peaceful blue sky turned grey, and the more the women chanted the darker the sky grew and the wind began to blow becoming stronger and stronger. The disturbing sounds began to unsettle the soldiers. Within a few moments the wind had kicked up enough dust from the ground that they could no longer see the Lithmorian army. Thunder and lightning began to erupt and finally the ground began to shake, Miska's horse spooked, she broke away from her chanting in an attempt to calm the frightened animal, two of the soldiers rushed to her side grabbing the reins in an attempt to calm the frightened creature.

Both women were now in a trance like state oblivious to anything around them, their eyes appeared red with fire. The soldiers that accompanied them knew that their Queen and Miska were capable of magic but they had never before witnessed anything like this and although they were brave men they found themselves terrified. Cynthiana's cape flapped in the wind her white hair almost glowed in the grey light as the noise of the thunder and lightning became so loud and violent that the men feared for their lives, the two men holding onto the horse's lost their own mounts as the poor creatures were so startled they bolted off into the distance. The soldiers stood rigid with fear as they witnessed both Miska and Cynthiana eyes begin to shoot rays of light spurting upwards like fireworks.

followed by a tremendous bang and out of the sky they could see a huge lightning bolt shoot down to the ground causing such a thud, the ground convulsed. Miska's horse was so frightened it reared knocking the soldiers to the ground leaving Miska holding on for dear life and it was only by luck and Miska's good horsemanship she managed to stay mounted until she could calm the terrified animal. Cynthiana too had been knocked to the ground by the force of energy that had impacted the earth, she now picked herself up and began to brush the dust from her. They had all felt the surge of heat as the thunder bolt hit the ground, but now all that remained was silence, the shaking had stopped, the dark clouds had all disappeared and they could all now clearly see the results of their endeavour.

A huge crevice, so deep into the earth that no man nor beast could ever cross it. They had succeeded in stopping the Lithmorian army, they were never going to get across that. If they wanted to reach Maro now they would have to find another way. Cynthiana and Miska began to laugh and with them the soldiers that had accompanied them although they laughed more out of relief that they had survived the ordeal. They could see in the far distance that the cloud of dust had settled telling them that the Lithmorian army was no longer marching forward.

The two women stood admiring their work while the horses were rounded up. They had succeeded in stopping the Lithmorian army from invading Maro now they must concentrate on destroying the stone and there was no time to lose as they were both convinced Inna would be eager to recapture the stone. For now thought Cynthiana the army could return to Maro. It was going to take the Lithmorian army weeks to find an alternative route into Maro and by that time it would be too late. Inna would be dead the stone would be no more and she would be Queen of Lithmore and the mines would belong to her but more than that, she thought, more than all the gold, or land. she would have power and for Cynthiana that was what she craved the most. As for Miska it was all about the gold. she dreamt about gold, for years she thought of nothing else. When she was a young dwarf many years ago, she remembered being told tales of the Lithmorian gold mines. It was her people who had first discovered them and it was her people who had mined them many, many years ago, so the story goes. but as always greedy humans got involved and tried to steal the gold, this angered the dwarfs who decided if they could not have the gold no one would, so they hid all the caves so that no man could ever find them and left them lay hidden for centuries passing down the knowledge of their whereabouts from generation to generation through one line of the dwarf clang and that line was the Maroos of which Miska belonged to, in fact she was the only living Maroo left. She had made it her life's work to get herself into a position so that one day she could regain the mines by whatever means it would take no matter what she had to go through or what she had to do in order to succeed. Humans on the whole hated dwarfs they did not trust or like them and Miska knew this, had she attempted to find the mines on her own she knew she would have been dead long ago even with her magic. she knew there were enough people out there who also had magic and enough hatred for her kind that without the protection of Cynthiana her chances were slim.

However she had been clever and patient which is not a characteristic of a dwarf in general but in her case she had managed it, she had befriended the King and Queen gaining their trust. Delighting them with a potion to help them conceive a much desired child, a child that Miska groomed for her own means, teaching her in the ways of magic, to despise all humans in the same way that she did. Guiding her every step. Miska could not help smiling to herself as she recalled how easy it was to kill the King, making Cynthina Queen and forever her protector. No one would dare try to harm her while under the protection of her Queen. Her only regret was she had not managed to get rid of Delphine, but she felt sure the opportunity would arise in the near future to remedy that.

The small party rode back to Maro at a leisurely pace. Cynthiana and Miska rode side by side quietly discussing ways of destroying the stone. In the distance up ahead they could see a horseman racing towards them. Stopping, the women watched the young soldier as he brought his horse to an abrupt halt in front of them and dismounted with such speed leaving both women in no doubt that he was bringing bad news. Cynthiana let out a deep sigh.

'Now what?'

The young man bowed down in front of Cynthiana.

'Your majesty, I have been sent to tell you, your mother Queen Delphine has been spotted in the palace.'

Cynthiana was so outraged to hear these words she kicked her foot out at the young man knocking him to the ground.

'First of all, she is not the Queen. I am and second,' but then she found herself lost for words.

'Why, oh why has she not been dealt with before now?' her face began to burn with rage.

'Were is she? has she been arrested? and is that idiot Kadar with her?'

She sat on her mount glaring down at the now petrified messenger.

'Well speak up you moron.'

'No your majesty, I don't think so, I don't know, just your mother.'

'And have you arrested her?'

The young soldier shook sensing his life was in mortal danger, he knew his answer was not going to please his raging Queen.

'No your majesty.'

'Arrrrgh you stupid moron,' and with that she reared her stallion up bringing the horses hoof crashing down onto the innocent messenger clipping the side of his head, causing the poor young man to collapse in a heap on the ground. Without any regard, Cynthiana instructed her horse to move on leaving the injured soldier bleeding and badly injured.

'Come on Miska you can bet if my mother is there so are the others.'

Dam that Inna, thought Miska were they ever going to be rid of these thorns.

Cythinana whipped her horse forcing him on, the others followed until the rumbling sound of horses hoofs galloping filled the air as everyone began to rush back to the palace. When they finally reached the gates of Maro the horses snorting and out of breath completely exhausted and virtually near collapse. Cynthiana dismounted screaming orders even before her feet had touched the ground. She raced up the steps into the large hall. Behind her two soldiers were anxiously helping Miska down from her mount she shouted loudly at them in her eagerness to keep up with her Queen. Finally reaching the ground she raced her little stubby legs up the steps into the hall huffing and puffing until she reached Cynthiana's side. One of the chief guards came running through the large hall towards them.

‘Have you found her yet?’ Cynthiana screamed.

The breathless guard spoke.

‘Forgive me your Majesty, but most of the men do not know your mother is an enemy of the state. There are only a handful of us who are aware of the situation and it was one of these men who informed me, she was here and as soon as I knew, I sent a messenger to you. We have been looking for her ever since, with no success. but we are pretty sure she is still here.’

Miska and Cynthiana looked at each other they knew exactly where they could find them.

‘Gather some men and follow us.’

With no time to lose they quickly made their way to the corridor with the secret doorway down to the Living Stone.

CHAPTER NINETEEN

Luck was on their side because for once Calem had managed to transport everyone precisely into Delphine's old chambers, Zelda noticed a glimmer of triumph in Calem's eyes and smiled discretely to herself. They stood a good chance of reaching the cave from this room as they could travel almost anyway in the palace from here, using the secret doorway into the hidden passages.

These tunnels had been built as escape routes for the Kings and Queens in times of conflict and although Delphine had never known them to be used for escape she and Kadar had often used them to spy on Cynthiana who had never been given the secret of them.

Inna's breathing began to rattle. Teka shot a worried look to Zelda who said.

'We must hurry,' Then turning to Calem she whispered.

'I am frightend.'

'Keep strong my sweet.'

Delphine and Kadar had already began to move some furniture away from the wall on which hung a huge tapestry of a picture of the city and its people in happier times, the artist had depicted the old King and Queen happily mingling with the people of Maro. For one split second Delphine stared at the picture, remembering a time gone by, and felt a twinge of sadness at the loss of those happier days, then Kadar yanked the picture aside to reveal a door suddenly jolting Delphine's thoughts back to the present. Turning to face everyone she said.

'We can follow this passage it will take us to the north side where we need to be, when we arrive, we will be exposed as we will have to come out of one passage into a main corridor to enter the tunnel to the cave. There will be guards I am sure.'

'Well we will need a plan before we get there then.' Calem was holding Inna close to him aided by Teka who was not very happy he was not the one holding her.

'We need a diversion.' piped in Kadar.

'Good idea,' agreed Calem passing Inna to Teka to hold.

'It only takes one of us to take Inna to the stone.' added Zelda.

'And I think it should be Calem, because he is the only one who has a chance of saving Inna and rescuing the stone.'

'Yes, yes your quite right.' They all agreed.

'Delphine will open the door to the secret passage to allow Calem to reach the cave,. The rest of us must cause the diversion.'

Kadar being a military man was now in his element and keen to take the lead he knew the tunnels better than anyone. A plan had been made and with that Teka returned Inna to Calem and one by one they entered into the dark corridor and began to make their way to the north side of the palace. The space was very narrow and dark but their eyes soon adjusted as a little light seeped through the cracks in the wall helping them to see. Cobwebs filled the passageways Kadar wiped them away and disregarded them as they clung to his bare arms.

They had managed to walk some way when suddenly they heard voices. They all came to an abrupt halt for fear of being heard. Inna let out a gentle whimper. they all held they breath fearing they were about to be discovered.

'What was that?' They heard one voice say.

'What was what?' said another.

Everyone's eyes met. no one daring to move, or breath, they could not do anything about Inna but they were all willing her to remain silent.

'Oh it was nothing,' the first voice finally said.

'Do you think Cynthiana will succeed in permanently stopping the Lithmorian army?' continued the other voice.

'Oh she will succeed all right, she has the devil in her and the devil at her side in the shape of Miska.'

Both the men began to laugh.

'Come on. There is nothing to concern ourselves here, let's get back to the others.'

The sound of footsteps trailed off into the distance.. Everyone breathed a sigh of relief.

'Wow that was close.'

Although riddled with fear for Inna's safety there was a part of Teka that was excited by the danger. His adrenaline was running high, he was keen to continue.

Kadar once again took the lead. Delphine had been correct the corridor that hid the secret door to the cave was heavily guarded, Delphine doubted very much if the guards knew why they were there or even what they were guarding. Cynthiana was a true royal in that sense. The only people that knew about the secret door and how to open it where of royal blood although she suspected that Miska may have been given that knowledge, horrible creature, thank goodness, thought Delphine, that they did not know of the other tunnels throughout the palace. Her husband had been wise when he decided to decline that knowledge to Cynthiana.

Teka was now looking through a small gap and could see several men, some chatting to each other, others appeared to be playing a game. all seemed to be quite relaxed.

'Right, this is where we split up.' Calem was speaking as softly as possible.

‘You all know what you have to do.’

Everyone nodded their heads. Kadar squeezed Delphine’s arm and gently pulled her to him kissing the back of her head. Delphine was shocked Kadar had never before done such a thing and even though they were in this dark small little space up to their necks in danger she could not help but feel a tingle of pleasure rise up her spine, she turned her head to face him but he had already gone.

‘Be safe.’ She whispered after him.

Next to leave was Teka and Zelda.

It seemed an eternity that Calem and Delphine stood quietly waiting for the others to make their move. They watched the guards through the peep hole when 'Dong, Dong, Dong,' The guards all stopped what they were doing and sprung into action. Delphine and Calem could hear raised voices amidst the men. Delphine heard one of them shout fire and like a stampede of wild animals all the guards rushed out of the corridor leaving the secret passageway unattended. Calem and Delphine looked at each other and smiled,

‘They did it. Come on, we may not have much time.’ Calem picked Inna up from the ground where he had lain her and he and Delphine quickly crossed the hallway to the secret door.

Successfully inserting the code Define quickly unlocks the door.

‘May speed be on your side and you reach the stone in time.’

Calem just nodded his head and with that he vanished around the door moving as fast as he was able, the air smelt dank and cool to Calem's nostrils. He could not help but wonder how the others were doing, were they all safe, had Delphine managed to return to the secret tunnel without being seen, and what of Zelda and Teka would they find their way back to their meeting place. Enough of this, thought Calem, he must concentrate on getting Inna to the stone.

These were not manmade tunnels he was now in but natures doing. As he looked around he was able to see, thanks to Cynthiana who had placed touches along the route. There were several paths but only one that was lit so he chose to follow that one and hurried along. As he travelled he appeared to be going deeper and deeper into the earth descending all the time. It became difficult to maneuver around the rocks and he slipped, desperately he held onto Inna who remained motionless in his arms. Finally the ground became more even and the path less difficult. Now he could see clearly ahead of him, In the near distance a dim light flickered. Squinting he tried to focus his eyes. Was that the stone up ahead, he was not sure but then the closer he got he could see that yes, yes, at last he had found it. just a few more steps and he would be there. He began to run with Inna firmly in his arms until he reached the Living Stone. Gently he laid her down upon it.

‘Please, please,’ he said out loud.

‘Don't let it be too late.’

Staring down at her lifeless body he feared she had stopped breathing, her face void of colour, he placed his ear over her mouth to reassure himself she was still breathing. Good he thought, she still has life. In that moment he heard the sound of swords being drawn, his heart leapt, quickly he turned around to face two guards, unarmed, what chance had he against two men waving swords at him, thoughts began racing around in his mind to find a solution to this critical situation. For the first time in his life he felt real fear, beads of sweat began falling down his forehead, he could not see an escape. Then to his surprise one of the guards Looking past Calem and at straight at Inna said.

‘That is the girl we saw, the vision.’

‘Is she real?’ said the other.

‘Touch her and see.’

Ignoring Calem, they crept towards the stone and Inna but then jumped back hysterically when the stone burst into life. The whole cave seemingly coming to life. Inna's body shot into the air and hung in suspension. All three men startled, watched in amazement as the young girl began to float and dance in the air above the stone, swirling colours swished and swirled around her. The sound of singing began to fill their ears, none of them had ever heard anything so exquisite or beautiful, not even Calem when he had first seen Inna in the healing chamber. All three men stood mesmerised as they watched in awe. Inna was glowing, her eyes now open and she was smiling down at the three spellbind men.

'Who are you?' the first guard finally managed to speak.

Still smiling, Inna replied.

'I am Inna, keeper of the Living Stone, this stone.' They stared at it, entranced, they could see energy pulsating from it and the glorious colours surrounding the aura of the stone. the two guards knew instinctively that this was something very, very precious indeed and that Inna was a very special person.

'Wow.' Both the guards responded, then the second guard straightened up and said.

'That's all very well, but we are here to guard that stone.

'Cynthiana will have our lives if we let anything happen to this or you in fact. We have to take you prisoners.'

'Oh dear, I don't think that is necessary do you. is that what you really want to do with us?'

'Well no, but we don't want to die either, and if we let you go that is what is going to happen.'

Inna thought for a moment, then looking in the eyes of these two young men, she thought they did not look like killers, they certainly did not want to take them prisoners she could see it in their hearts, they only wanted the best for her but she understood their fear for Cynthiana was justified. She would surely kill them if they allowed them to escape. What was to be done? how could she help them.

'Let me ask you this, if you obey your orders what will your rewards be.'

Both men looked at each other and shrugged their shoulders.

'There will not be any rewards.' said the first guard.

'In fact the chances are we will have done something wrong and we will get punished or even worse, she is a terrible, cruel Queen.' spoke the second hanging his head, ashamed of admitting how wicked his Queen was.

'Well then, if you help me, I promise, I will help you and we will take you back to Lithmore with us. we can do that can't we Calem.'

Calem was still soaking up the lovely energies from the Living Stone and was feeling somewhat dazed.

'Oh yes.' he agreed, although he would have agreed to almost anything in that moment.

'Very well this is what we need to do.'

*****

Delphine was surprised to see the guard appear from around the corner as she made her way back to the secret tunnel, she quickly sidestepped into a room hoping that she had not been seen. Her heart thumped so hard in her chest that the sensation resonated up to her head pulsating into her ears, quickly she scanned the room for a safe place to hide, she knew there was no way to reach a secret passage from this room, she was trapped, the footsteps were getting louder and there was more than one voice she could hear. Without a doubt she knew she must have been seen. For a moment she panicked, there was nowhere to hide then she saw the fireplace and ran towards it as fast as she could and quickly crawled into the back of it and found a ledge were she was able to stand on. The door burst open into the room, every fibre in her body froze.

'She must be in here somewhere. I could have sworn I saw her come in here.'

'Well where is she?' said an older sterner voice.

'Rip this place apart you stupid imbecile,' commanded the stern voice.

Delphine could hear banging and furniture moving, lots of cursing until finally the stern voice spoke again.

'You must have been dreaming man there is nothing here, you did not see anything.

Come on let us see how the others are getting on with putting the fire out.'

Delphine waited a few minutes until it was silent then allowed herself to breathe a sigh of relief, she was safe, for now at least. but she still had to get back to the secret tunnel unnoticed.

CHAPTER TWENTY

'Well, well. Who do we have here?'

Delphine froze, trapped like a wild animal, her heart began to beat so fast she knew there was no escape. She turned to face her daughter. Just one second more and she would have been safely out of site. As it was she stood alone, with no hope of rescue. She faced Cynthiana and that evil twisted little Miska with a gang of guards standing behind them. Delphine released a defeated sigh.

Zelda and Teka managed to reach the meeting place and were now looking through the peep hole, both clinging to each other for support not daring to breath or move for fear of being discovered. Both silently desperately trying to think of a way to help Delphine as they watched in horror.

'Arrest her.' instructed Cynthiana.

'We will deal with her later.'

Delphine gazed at the young women before her and did not recognise a trace of her own essence about her. How, she thought, could this stranger be my child, so cruel, where was the kindness of her father, the humanity. It was as if the same blood did not run through her veins.

'We will deal with her now.' said Miska.

And before Cynthiana could utter another word, Miska pointed her little bony staff at Delphine, who's eyes widened, as she realised her moment had come.

'dah lee gar ma.' shouted Miska.

A bolt of lightning shot from her staff and knocked Delphine dead to the ground. Zelda's sharp intake of breath was immediately followed by fear that she had been heard but the shock and anger on Cynthiana's face told her she had not, as she heard her scream.

'You did not have the right to do that, that is my place to decide who lives or dies.'

Cynthiana felt no sorrow for her mother's death but she was furious that Miska had countermanded her orders.

'Well it is done now and we are wasting time.'

Miska was adding even more fuel to the fire by continuing to undermine Cynthiana in front of the guards and she began to seethe, flashes of being used as a puppet came to mind once more as she furiously glared at Miska. Then remembering their mission she quickly pushed her thoughts aside, she would deal with her later, for now she needed Miska but later when all this was over she promised herself that Miska would understand that she and she alone was ruler of Maro and of Lithmore when they eventually conquer it and as for the mines they would be hers alone. Yes, she thought, Miska needed to be taught a lesson.

'Remove the body.' Miska instructed.

'Leave it.' snapped Cynthiana taking control.

'We have more important things to attend to.'

And with that said she turned toward the secret panel and led the way into the cave.

Kadar arrived back at the meeting place to find Zelda quietly sobbing, confused he was led by Teka gently to the peep hole so that he could see the cause of her grief. Immediately his heart sank as his eyes beheld the crumbled lifeless figure of Delphine lying on the ground. His heart leapt into his throat and a tightness grabbed his chest. He had to get to her and he had to get to her now, not caring if there were any guards around he rushed through into the cold bare corridor hastily followed by Zelda and Teka. He collapsed to his knees beside Delphine's dead body picking her up cradling her in his arms, he held her so close to him. In all the years he had served her, in all the years he had loved and adored her he had never been this close to her, his Queen his friend. He thought his heart would break as the tears fell down upon her cheeks.

'Kadar, we must go, it is too dangerous here.' Teka was speaking softly, pleading with Kadar.

'We are too exposed.'

'I can't leave her, I can't.' The strong man they all knew appeared to have crumbled.

Kadar could not bear the thought of leaving Delphine here in Maro he wanted her with him wherever that may be. Zelda gently tapped his shoulder.

'Bring her with you, we will manage.'

He gently raised her in his strong arms.

'I did not know.' Zelda said.

Kadar coughed and sniffed fighting back the tears.

'No,' he looked into Delphine's beautiful face.

'Neither did she.'

Zelda felt the tears fall down her face, how sad she felt to lose such a friend but even sadder for Kadar to have loved her and for her never to have known it. Just then as they were deciding which way to go, two small figures appeared in the corridor, immediately the three prepared themselves for conflict but quickly realised that the figures were that of two small children, as they got closer they recognised them as Ni and Klio the Children of Vision they looked almost transparent. For a moment they all just stared at one another not believing what the other was seeing.

'Hello you two, what brings you here.' Zelda spoke first.

Ni and Klio smiled and pointed to the cave entrance.

'Why don't they answer you.' asked Teka.

'There not really here remember, they have astral travelled here, they are trying to tell us something.'

'Do you want us to go to the cave where Inna is.' asked Teka.

Both the children nodded and smiled. Kadar was still holding Delphine in his arms, Ni stepped forward and touched Delphine's cheek, then again he indicated that they go to the cave.

'But if Calem has succeeded they will be back at Lithmore and all we will find is Cynthiana and her soldiers, it will be like walking into a trap.' Protested Teka.

Ignoring Teka, Ni and Klio motioned once again that they go to the cave. Suddenly the entrance to the cave opens.

'I think we should do as they say, do you both agree?'

Zelda always went on her gut instinct and her guts were telling her this was the thing to do. Both Kadar and Teka agreed which delighted the children who both clasped their hands together and gave a little bow and as if they had completed their mission they faded into nothingness leaving the small group to carry out their instructions.

*****

There was no time to make a plan, the look on the young guards faces told Inna that they had all heard something. They turned their attention to the entrance of the cave in the distance, sure enough they could hear the sound of footsteps and lots of them.

'We can escape, come on Inna, we must get out of here now.'

Calem finally in control of his senses was eager to escape.

'But the others, they are still here somewhere in the palace, I am not leaving without them.' insisted Inna.

'We can come back for them, now come on.' Calem insisted.

The two young shoulders glanced back and forth from Calem to Inna as they spoke, clearly becoming more concerned as each second past, they knew if Cynthiana caught them, they were certainly going to die.

'No, we have to stay and face them.'

There was a determination in Inna's voice, she had made her mind up. one of the young guards moaned in desperation. Inna did not know how she was going to save them but something deep inside her told her she must stay and face this once and for all. Turning to Calem and the two young guards she could see fear, concern, and panic in their eyes. The sound of the footsteps got louder and closer.

'Trust me.' she paused for a moment.

'Now stand back.'

She inhaled a deep breath and grabbed her crystal from around her neck and jumped upon the Living Stone. She began to call for her Grandmother, she closed her eyes hoping upon hope that what her Grandmother had promised her was true, that when she really needed her she would come, she would come and help her, well now was the time, she squeezed her eyes tight.

In the distance she could hear Cynthiana's voice they had arrived at the entrance of the cave . Inna opened her eyes to see the raging anger on Cynthiana's face for one brief moment their eyes met.

Cynthiana opened her palms and out of them came bolts of lightning shooting towards Inna and the others but to everyone's surprise the lightning rebounded as though it hit a wall. The attackers dived to the ground. Miska and Cynthiana exchanged glances, Miska tried with her staff and the same thing happened. Cynthiana then gave the order for the guards to charge but they were forced back. All the time Inna stood tall on top of the Living Stone with her crystal in her hand calling for her Grandmother. Inna could feel her feet begin to vibrate as the ground began to rumble. Inna could see that Cynthiana and Miska were now holding hands merging their magic shouting out words she could not understand over and over again getting louder and louder, rocks began to fall. Helplessly she watched as the guards once again tried to force through the energy barrier this time succeeding they rushed towards Calem and the two guards grabbing them, bravely they tried to fight them off but there were too many of them and within seconds they were overwhelmed, Inna's heart raced, this can't be, she thought, we cannot lose, please Grandmother where are you? Inna held onto the crystal as she watched the guards force Calem and the two young guards to the ground she could hardly bare to look, would they be killed right before her eyes. To her horror she could see Cynthiana and Miska laughing as they now moved in on her, the victors, they were now so close that she looked down onto their smug faces, she was defeated, how could this be, she had truly believed her Grandmother would come, she had believed with every cell of her being. But it was clear to Inna that she was defeated the only thing ahead of her was humiliation and execution, oh no, she thought my friends they will all suffer the same fate. oh Grandmother how could you desert me so. Miska began to laugh,

‘See how brave she is now, with tears running down her face.’

‘And to think she has caused us all this trouble, get down from that stone.’ Cynthiana snarled.

She reached up to grab poor Inna but as she did so a sharp jolt knocked her backwards launching both Cynthiana and Miska to the ground. The guards drew back releasing the three men as they stared at the stone with astonished looks upon their faces. The stone had burst into life, Inna who had been standing on the stone was now suspended high above it, everyone looked up and could see that she was not alone. There beside her were a host of women. Inna's Grandmother and her ancestors, they had come, they had come. The whole of the cave was ablaze with light and colour almost blinding to the eye. The guards felt this was some universal intervention and became frightened quickly drawing back.

'Stay where you are you cowards.' Cynthiana screamed.

She had no intentions of letting this situation intimidate her. She quickly regained her composure and tried to release a bolt of lightning towards Inna and the group of shimmering women, but nothing happened, she tried again but failed. swinging around to Miska she ordered her to try but she too failed.

'It's no use, ' A voice said.

'Your magic ceases to have power in our presence.'

Miska could see her beloved mines slipping away from her. This magic was more powerful than anything she knew. Pointing to Cynthiana.

'Please, She made me do it, it was her, she wanted Lithmore for herself, she wanted Inna dead.'

Cynthiana knocked her to the ground.

'You little traitor.' she began kicking and punching Miska.

'Stop.' Alannis was speaking.

Cynthiana paused for a moment and stared at Alannis.

'What are you going to do, you are just peacemakers, I know who you are. You are the Keepers of the Living Stone. You can't harm or stop me. go away.' and with that she proceeded to punch Miska.

'No but I can, and I have the power to do so.'

Cynthiana and Miska instantly froze as they recognised the voice. There in front of them stood the shimmering figure of a man. It was the King, Cynthiana's father. Cynthiana took one look at him and the blood drained from her face.

'No, no it can't be. it is not possible you lot are all dead.' she spluttered.

'Of course it is possible you have just chosen to believe it is not.'

The Kings voice was stern.

'But I have not come to talk to you about the mysteries of life I have come to finally make my kingdom a safe place from you and that thing besides you.'

The King stood erect with his arms crossed as he continued.

'The Living Stone is from another universe as are the origins of the Keepers of the Stone. It is a far more advanced universe than you can ever imagine. There are laws there as there are here and you two have broken many of them. It is true the Keepers of the Stone are a peaceful entity therefore your lives will be spared but I have been empowered to banish you to Leanter Sipron.'

The two women stared in disbelief Leanter Sipron was the worst place on earth stuck out in the middle of the ocean.

'You can't do that,' screamed Cynthiana.

'Oh but I can.'

Cynthiana began to shake, she looked around the cave for an escape but there was none. All eyes were upon them both.

'Before I send you. Is there anything you wish to say.'

'Go to hell.' Spat Miska.

'You can't do this to us, please farther,' pleaded Cynthiana.

'I am afraid you are the makers of your own destiny.'

Cynthiana looked down at her hands and could see them begin to fade, into nothingness.

'Please, please, farther,' she begged.

but it was too late, both woman vanished, banished forever to

Leanter Sipron.

The King having completed his task also faded and was gone.

'Our job here is also complete, you have done well my child.'

Inna looked at her beloved Grandmother. she had now become detached from the group and was now standing on the ground looking up at the group of woman.

'Thank you. I miss you Grandmother.'

'I know child, but you know I am always close by.'

And then she and the others were gone. Leaving the soldiers confused. Inna could not believe it, finally, they had managed to save the Living Stone, prevent Cynthiana and Miska from stealing the mines and rescued Lithmore, now all that was left was to find everyone and return home and to Hiliron.

Calem was smiling from ear to ear as he embraced Inna.

'We did it little one, we did it, now to find the others.' just as his words left his mouth

Zelda and Teka appeared followed by Kadar who was carrying the lifeless Delphine.

'Delphine.' Inna cried.

'Oh no.' echoed Calem.

All the guards turned towards Kadar and immediately knelt in respect as they could see their Queen was no more.

Inna sighed deeply. No this cannot be, thought Inna. Kadar stood in front of her, the devastation on Kadar's face clear, Inna had never seen grief this close up before.

'You are the keeper of the stone.' said a voice.

'What!'

'You are the keeper of the stone.' There it was again, Inna swung around, it was the stone speaking to her.

'Quick.' Inna instructed.

'Lay her onto the stone.'

'But it is impossible.' Kadar protested.

'Do as I say.' commanded Inna.

Everyone stood aside, Kadar gently laid Delphine onto the Living Stone. Everyone stared in anticipation, the stone began to convulse with light shooting up making it impossible to see Delphine. With loud cracking sounds the Stone seemed to be shrieking a noise that Inna had never heard before, then the light went out and the noises stopped leaving the stone with just a gentle glow. There was silence in the cave, everyone was transfixed on Delphines body but nothing, she still lay lifeless. The stone had done nothing. Inna's heart sank. What was she expecting anyway.

Kadar moved closer now to touch Delphine's hand he needed to be close to her.

'I want to take her back to Tori Plains, she loved it there, that is where I shall rest her body.'

'Yes, yes of course.' Everyone agreed.

'Not just yet you won't,' came a weak little voice.

Kadar shot his head around to find Delphine's eyes open. She was alive, in that moment he thought he would explode with joy. He could not believe what he was witnessing. She was alive. The stone had done the impossible, it had really managed to bring

Delphine back to them. Everyone was so overjoyed, Inna and Teka swung around like small children, Calem and Zelda fell into a passionate kiss and Kadar forgot all protocol and wrapped his arms around Delphine hugging her close to him in a firm embrace gently caressing her lips with his. Joy and laughter filled the air. Finally, thought Inna all is well, we can all go home.

*****

Several months had passed since the return of the Living Stone and today Delphine and Kadar were visiting Lithmore.

‘I can't wait until Delphine and Kadar arrive.’

Inna was almost a child again she was so in excited. Calem and Zelda, Teka and Hiliron were all here it was going to be such a lovely reunion.

‘Would that be us you are talking about then.’ Inna turned around to see her dear friends,

she ran towards them flinging her arms around their necks.

‘ How lovely to see you. We have missed you so much.’

It was wonderful, they were all together again. Delphine and Kadar had spent the last several months helping Maro's citizens build a better life for themselves.

‘At last, we are all together again. the people I love most, Hiliron we should make a toast, raise a glass to the friends we made along the way, even funny old Harmeni and of course dear, dear Ni and Klio who without their help I certainly would not be here today.’

‘Talking of which.’ interrupted Teka.

‘Didn't they say if one day they needed us for some reason your crystal would go red.’

‘That's right, we made that a signal, if they should ever need our help the crystal would turn red and we would know that they needed our help immediately.’

'It's gone red.' They all shouted in unison.

The End

Authors bio

Katie Lives in the heart of beautiful Suffolk with her Husband Peter. She has had an ongoing love affair with crystals since a child and through the years has taught and practiced crystal therapy to many people.

Printed in Great Britain
by Amazon